FALLEN ANGEL

Angels and Demons, Book One

SKYLAR WEST

Published by Eclipse Press
An Imprint of
ABCD Graphics and Design, Inc.
A Virginia Corporation
977 Seminole Trail #233
Charlottesville, VA 22901

Skylar West
Fallen Angel

Amazon ISBN: 978-1-64563-581-9
Barnes & Noble ISBN: 978-1-64563-582-6
Kobo ISBN: 978-1-64563-583-3
Apple ISBN: 978-1-64563-584-0
Print ISBN: 978-1-64563-585-7
Audio ISBN: 978-1-64563-586-4
v1

Chapter 1

Isabelle

Our band was on a break when I received a drink from an admirer. Unlike a typical fruity cocktail, or worse, a beer, this admirer sent a glass of champagne. A brand, the bar we are playing does not stock. I lifted the delicate flute and took my first sip. It was pure deliciousness. Closing my eyes, I let the taste carry me away. I moaned at the pleasure on my tongue, knowing the sound I emitted was drowned out by the club's pounding music, the sounds of laughter and loud talking.

When I looked around to see whom my admirer was, my eyes landed on him. A ruggedly handsome face with intelligent eyes watched me intently, and his lips lifted in a smug smile. I felt a tug deep down in my core. I would have to watch out for this one; he spelled trouble with a capital T.

He did not approach me, and I did not invite him over to join me. I was going to chalk up this new admirer to an intriguing, but intimidating prospect and hope he would leave by the end of the night.

When our final set ended, I left with my fellow band members, Steve and Marshall. My admirer was nowhere in sight. I sighed and made my way up to my darkened studio at peace. My relief was short-lived. The next night, my admirer was there, and each night that week.

We began a courtship dance of sorts. I hated to admit, but I began to look forward to seeing my admirer. On my break, he would send me an exotic drink that my taste buds would welcome, delighting my pallet every night. I would toast him from across the room, acknowledging his gift but not inviting him over.

The man, whose name I learned from the bartender, was Iver. He looked like an Iver, tall, dark and handsome, probably 6'4" with dark Anglo-Saxon features and bright blue eyes that glittered in the darkness of the club. He had quite the physique, not massive, but sculpted, and he was a total predator.

It was the final night of our gig, and our band was out in the alley smoking a joint. I didn't usually indulge, been there and done that. As it was the last set of the night, I figured why not. After tonight, I had a week off until our next gig in Greenwich Village, and I was looking forward to it.

We were about to head back in when a gang of miscreants surrounded us; our three to their six were not good odds. Marshall and Steve stood in front of me; being the only girl in either group, I guess they thought this made me vulnerable. Little did they know, I'd been taking taekwondo for years. Being single and a band girl out late at night, I'd signed up for classes at the suggestion of my brother Finn.

It had been a good suggestion.

I was moving into a fighting stance when Iver and another man of more enormous proportions stepped out of the back door and into the alley, flanking us. The pack got the hint and moved away, loping down the lane in the opposite direction.

Iver introduced himself and his friend, Raphe, to Steve and Marshall. After shaking hands, they headed inside. Following the guys into the safety of the club, Iver asked if he could speak with me for a moment. Steve glanced back, checking to see if I was okay. I nodded, and he continued in the door, following Raphe and Marshall, the three of them talking and joking around like old friends.

"Isabelle," Iver said. And the way he said my name sent shivers down my spine to my knees. His voice was deep but not harsh. It soothed and invited me into his space. I felt compelled and knew he was not a simple admirer.

I gazed into the light blue ice chips that were his eyes. They seemed like endless glacier pools, but they held no malice in them, the very opposite was true. His eyes were smoldering with passion, fiery passion.

How could that be? I didn't know the man. What could I have done to ignite such passion? I prided myself on being a good judge of character, but he was such a contradiction. One thing I did know that what I was seeing and what was real, were not the same things. My instincts wanted me to run, while a completely different side wanted to know this man.

"Who protects you, Isabelle?"

Say what? I was so engrossed in my thoughts that I almost missed his question. Who protected me? I protected me, of course, but I got the feeling that was not the answer he was asking. "I have two brothers," I finally answered, wondering where his line of questioning was going.

"And where are they?" he asked gently.

"Living their lives," I said with an edge, "and I don't see how it's any of your business?"

He frowned; maybe he was not used to an outspoken woman. Or perhaps he thought I was rude. Either way, I didn't care. He'd hit a trigger; who protects me? Really? What the hell was that?

"You need someone in your life, a protector, someone to keep you safe and in line," he added with a small grin, his twin pools emitting a strange light that I had not noticed before.

Despite his teasing, my body felt that sensation again, molten lava right down to my core, making my knees weak, almost giving out from the power of his words. Iver wasn't speaking to my intelligence; he was talking to my psyche, what made me tick. I had no doubt what being my protector meant with Iver.

Suddenly having a vision of me being held in his arms, seeing him drive me to gigs and seeing him watching me, always watching me, from the corners of the smoky clubs I was playing, I had a shiver run down my spine and shook it off.

"That may be, but I have raised myself and have no problem dealing with whatever comes along. It was nice to meet you, Iver, but I must get back inside."

I headed in the door, feeling his eyes on my back until the door swung closed. I blew out my breath, feeling as if I had just undergone a battle and not sure I came out the victor. Now if I could only avoid him for the rest of the night. My hope was short-lived; when I re-entered the club, I spotted Raphe sitting with Marshall and Steve.

All three looked up at me, and then all three sets of eyes moved behind me in unison. He was behind me. Iver, I could feel his gaze; it was commanding, searing me to my core. My breath caught, and my body froze, I'm sure I looked like a deer caught in the headlights.

I was thankful when, in the next moment, the guys rose and headed to the stage. I followed and blew out another deep breath. At this pace, I would render myself unconscious if I kept holding my breath whenever I felt Iver's eyes on me.

"Hey, Isabelle, Raphe invited us to his friend's after-hours club, wanna join?"

I was about to decline when Marshall added, "Come on,

Isabelle, it won't be the same without you, and besides, this could be another potential gig for us; you've heard of Swank?"

I stopped in my tracks. "That BDSM club? You can't be serious?"

"Well, that's just the two bottom floors, Isabelle, the top two are insane. They hold a thousand people and have a track record of successful artists coming out of there with record deals. Raphe said that the recording industry giants are regulars; this could be a chance for us?"

My gut told me to run, but I was curious. How come the industry giants frequented that particular club? I knew it was known for being the largest club in New York City's west side. That alone would draw in the rich and famous. I'd heard that even Hugh Heffner had made it out to the opening and cut the ceremonial ribbon.

I never thought I would ever get in. I knew it had a waiting list a mile long, and the names that filled the list were not ordinary folks, like myself. "Yeah, yeah, don't get your panties in a twist; I'll tag along."

The guys and I were going to take a cab, but Raphe had his driver pick us up in a short limo. I had another moment of panic and almost didn't step inside the vehicle. Something told me that if I did, my life would be irrevocably changed.

I knew when we arrived, as the line-up down the street gave it away. Raphe's driver dropped us at the curb, directly opposite the red carpet. Two enormous men stood on either side. They both wore suits and sunglasses. I gazed at those glasses; they were not your typical nightshades. I think they had thermal imaging in them. Holy hell, how did I know that, and who were these guys to have thermal imaging?

I drew my gaze away from the two enormous doormen, undoing my seat belt. I was about to open the door when it opened for me. Raphe took my hand as I stepped out of the limo, his grip firm on mine. He gazed down at me from his massive height; he had to be close to six foot eight, his shoulders were so broad. Maybe he was a retired football player. But he looked so young, mid to late twenties; he shouldn't be an ex or retired anything at this point. If he were a professional athlete, he would be in his prime.

Iver waited until we had all exited the limo and stood on the red carpet, then linking my arm through his, we walked up the few stairs and into the club. My senses were assaulted from all angles once we stepped through the doors.

I was surprised by the size of the club. From the outside, one would never know how big and soundproof the building was. I had only felt the pulse of the music when I was just outside the doors, but inside, was entirely different.

The lights were dim, but not so dark that you couldn't see. Ahead, in what looked like a giant floating birdcage, were two D.J.s working the sound. The two-tiered dance floor was packed. And it wasn't with people all my age, either. The place drew an eclectic crowd, but one thing was evident by the appearance of the dancers, wealth. I doubted there was anyone of my financial caliber in the club.

I was suddenly aware of how I must look. Here were the guys and I, fresh off a gig, all leathered out with lots of dark make up, standing beside two incredibly gorgeous, rich men. I must have looked like a street rat in comparison.

I was about to tell the guys I was heading home when Iver leaned down to whisper in my ear. "Before you bolt, come and have a drink with me. If you go now, the guys may also leave, and maybe, you will all miss out on an opportunity."

His mouth so close to my ear sent chills down my spine. His voice was like a warm blanket. Whenever he spoke, I felt my body being wrapped by him. I think for your typical girl that would have been highly desirable. But for one who claimed independence and had done so at a high cost, not so much.

I prided myself on not needing anyone, especially one of

the opposite sex. Besides, both my brothers were overbearing already, so the thought of another one getting control of my life was as intolerable as the thought of wearing shackles. No, just no. But why not play along for tonight? A recording contract would be a welcomed event in my life.

Raphe led us to a table that was set apart and offered us an excellent viewing vantage. I loved people watching, and this was a perfect spot for it. I soon became engrossed with the activity around us.

There were some beautiful people here, especially women. Again, my street rat appearance crossed my mind. But as no one seemed to be noticing me, no pointing fingers at the Goth girl and her friends, I sat back and let it go. Did I care what a bunch of strangers thought of me?

No way, but did I care what Iver thought of me? I glanced in his direction; he was so good looking, it almost hurt to gaze at him. Okay, so maybe I cared a little, but he'd been watching me for nearly a week, and I'd looked as I did right now.

Raphe ordered drinks and shots. I can take a lot, so I pounded them back and had no problem requesting more. I wasn't paying the bill, so I didn't care, and this charade would end after tonight, so no harm, no foul as far as I was concerned.

At least that is what I told myself. My body, however, had an entirely different reaction. The longer I was seated beside Iver, the more my traitorous body wanted him. It was like he had specialty come-hither pheromones that attracted me, attacking my senses, and he seemed to know of my struggle.

Iver's lips ever so lightly brushed my earlobe as he spoke my name. "Isabelle, come dance with me."

I shrugged nonchalantly and let him guide me to the floor. *Therapy* came on, by Duke Dumont. A lazy smile lifted the left corner of my mouth. It was time to test Iver; could he dance? I mean, really dance? If he could, maybe I would give in to my attraction for him?

I let myself be free, sidling up to him. I turned around and ground my ass into his groin, which sprang to attention immediately. Ha, that would serve him to mess around with me. I swung back around and took in my dance partner.

He moved like a friggin' professional dancer without looking uptight. He wasn't performing, and he wasn't classically trained; it was natural. *Figures,* I huffed. The song changed. It wasn't a new one, but it was a redone one and the singer Michelle Kash was killing it.

I felt myself get taken over by the music, my eyes hooded as the sounds and vibrations resonated within me. I tried not to allow myself to let go too often. I knew that when I danced, it was like an elaborate seduction and I looked like a sex kitten.

Looking like a wanton nymph was unintentional. I just got lost in myself, and the world around me disappeared, the same as when I played drums. I often attracted unwanted attention. That was why I dressed the part of the Goth when we played. I had become very good at schooling myself to appear calm about everything. The better I was at remaining aloof, the better chance I had at avoiding uncomfortable situations.

What I looked like, and what I was, were very different. I'd never been comfortable with my looks. I felt they compromised me, and predators, like Iver, seemed to detect my uneasiness. Within seconds of letting go of my reserve, men surrounded us.

I mean, they made a circle around me, with Iver being one of them. He grinned like he thought it was a great game. I was surprised; a control freak would typically be getting into a fistfight by now. So, unhindered, I let go of all my inhibitions, dirty dancing with each in turn and letting myself go in a way I never had. I felt utterly safe, which was ridiculous, considering the men around me were all big and in excellent physical condition.

Despite my internal struggles and my uneasiness around men in general, I wanted this one. Watching Iver move was turning me on. I could feel the wetness between my legs and wondered if he knew the effect he had on me.

I spared a glance for Iver; his eyes glittered as he followed my every move. He wasn't jealous because he was arrogant and perfect. I was an idiot if I thought what I was doing would make him jealous. The game was no longer fun. I moved off the dance floor and back to my table, to find Marshall and Steve with a gaggle of young women hanging all over them.

I rolled my eyes and sat down, waving over a server. I ordered eight shots all for myself and lined them up, downing one after the other. I wanted to evoke a reaction in Iver, something to throw him off and change that confidant smirk into something less confidant. Acting as a brat had always worked well with my brothers.

Iver had rejoined me at the table by the time the shots arrived, and I stared into his eyes with a smirk on my face as I downed each one. I could tell my behavior was annoying him. I almost crowed with the momentary power I felt, moving the favor back from his court to mine.

A part of me was elated that I'd found a way to press his buttons. With the last shot downed, I turned it over on the table and looked at him with amusement. Let's see what the control freak would do now.

"Isabelle, I will escort you home."

It was a statement, not a question. "I'm perfectly happy to take a cab home, thank you."

He seemed to consider my words before responding. "You may be happy with that choice, but I am not, so I will escort you home and make sure you arrive safely." His voice dropped a few octaves so only I could hear what he said next. "And then we'll play another game."

I grinned, just what I expected from his personality. "Sure, you can escort me home. I live in a shitty little bachelor apartment. So, don't be expecting to enter a palace. My only passion is to play drums, and I don't care about where I live."

I don't know why I bothered to share that. I guess I was warning to have zero expectations when it came to me. When we arrived, I unlocked the door and invited Iver in. "Welcome to chez Isabelle," I joked. He took in the place at a glance; you could see the whole area from the entryway. Then he grabbed a chair and placed it in the middle of the one large room.

I grinned; this could prove to be an exciting game. I was tipsy, but not drunk. Most of the alcohol I consumed I'd burned off dancing, and the shots gave me only a momentary buzz. For some reason, I'd always been able to consume vast quantities of alcohol, and it rarely affected me. My brothers were the same, and for that reason, we usually didn't bother drinking much.

Tonight's indulging had been mainly to test Iver and enjoy some beverages that I couldn't afford with the pay I made. Living in New York costs a fortune.

"Isabelle, come to me."

I laughed; was he trying to compel me? My mind was enjoying the game; my body was giving away my true feelings, however, and I didn't know how long I would be able to deny them. Putting the chair in the center of the room had made me hotter than hell. My black thong was soaked, and I was beginning to feel an ache in my lady parts that needed addressing.

Maybe I could give in just this once and have sex with an actual person instead of the gadget I kept in my bedside table. "Why, Iver?" I purred. "Give me one reason to walk over to you."

He smiled in a way that made my core tighten and my knees go weak. "Isabelle, if you walk to me willingly, I will show you incredible pleasure. If you do not, you won't sit down for a week."

"What if I decide I don't want to play this game and wish you to leave; will you honor that?" It was suddenly essential to me that I chose what happened next and that he told me what I suspected was right, that he was an honorable man.

He sat back and regarded me, the twin pale pools of light like a beacon in the night, beckoning me. It was all I could do to stand my ground. I needed to know that whatever went down tonight, it happened with mutual consent.

"I can smell your excitement, Isabelle, drenched in your nectar. Your fragrance is intoxicating, like heaven, to my senses. I want to taste you to give you pleasure beyond anything you have ever experienced. Will you allow that?"

Oh god, I wanted to jump on his lap and never get off. But experience had taught me consensual sex was the only way to go. "I would like to, Iver, but I need your word, and I am recording it."

"Of course, Isabelle, I will honor your request. If at any time you want me to stop what I am doing, I will stop. If I feel your resistance, I will stop and ask again for your permission. Does that fulfill your requirements?" he smirked.

Damn him! The foreplay was over. Placing my phone down, I strutted over to Iver and sat down on his lap. His long, muscular legs were hard beneath my backside. I felt how strong they were through his expensive designer pants. I also felt his bulge, which felt enormous, and I hoped in proportion to the rest of his large, godlike body.

Suddenly feeling self-conscious, I asked, "How old are you, Iver?" I was not a good game player; I was too upfront, usually, for these types of things. If I liked someone, they knew it; if I didn't, I would tell them to fuck off. I was a straight-up girl.

Iver seemed to encourage keeping me on my toes, and I wasn't used to that. I had the very occasional hookup, and that was it. This thing between Iver and me, the chemistry, was beyond anything I 'd ever felt, and I hoped he proved to be as good as the game preceding it.

"As you have been a good girl, Isabelle, I will tell you anything you wish to know."

I giggled. "So if I'd been a bad girl, then what?"

"Then, I would have done this." Iver flipped me so quickly, it took me a moment to realize that I was face down over his lap. He had lightning speed reflexes; his hand came down on my backside in rapid succession. I sucked in my breath. He landed a few on my thighs where even my leather pants couldn't protect me from the sting his blows delivered.

Before I could squeak my protest, I was magically back upright. "But as you came to me of your own free will, you are spared a discipline spanking." His eyes danced with amusement.

I felt a series of emotions, shock, anger, amusement, turned on, and finally, vulnerable, and I didn't like that last one at all. "I am going to kiss you now, Isabelle, do I have your permission?"

I nodded, still reeling from the flurry of emotions that his spanking had sparked in me. As his lips closed over mine, I heard his words echo in my mind. 'Who protects you, Isabelle?'

Chapter 2

My kind had been wandering the earth for a long time, in search of redemption for past deeds. I was not one of the originals who fell, discarded from Heaven like yesterday's trash. I was a descendant of Enoch, God's celestial scribe, the keeper of knowledge. I guess that is why God was confused, yes, even the one true God can be jealous of his immortal siblings and children.

It was the record of intentions that Enoch had been working on that had landed him in trouble and eventually sent him to Earth. Enoch found shelter in a remote cave, in what would be known as Norway, where he stayed hidden for a thousand years.

One day at the river close to his cave, Enoch encountered a beautiful woman. She said her name was Freida and her people were all dead; she was tribeless and hungry. My father invited Freida into his cave. That night after feasting on fish and root vegetables, Enoch and Freida made love.

After they made love, Freida appeared as her goddess self,

Freya. She said she was with Enoch to help retain the fabric of magic among the human population, that many humans would come and destroy knowledge of the gods. She said that a child who was born part angel and part god was indestructible.

Freya stayed with my father in her human form, Freida, until her death. Their only child, me, male heir to the throne of their small kingdom, became my father's entire world. For two thousand years, we stayed hidden in the cold realms of what would one day be Norway.

When it was time to leave Norway, my father and I traveled to Africa, spending time amongst the deeply hidden tribes of the Congo. From there, we went to the Middle East and then to Russia. Eventually, in 500 AD we moved to what would be Europe, in the early days of England, long before it became a united island. We watched wars and witnessed entire groups of people annihilated. Kingdoms rose and fell. Through it all, my father was careful. We knew when to move on and start new. By the time the internet was blowing up around the world, we headed to the birthplace of the next phase in human evolution, Silicon Valley.

Chapter 3

Isabelle

I ver stared into my eyes; he was unreadable. His light glittering pools betrayed nothing of his thoughts, and his eyes had an unearthly quality to them that was more obvious in the dark. They glowed a little and not like a flashlight, more like moonlight.

He undid the zipper of my black leather pants. "Just say the word, Isabelle, and I will stop." He slid a finger into my wet folds. My breath hissed out as he found the hardened bud and pressed his thumb on it while continuing to stroke the wet petals surrounding it.

Stroking backward, he drew my slick juices up to the center of my ass. I felt my eyes widen in surprise. I was a virgin there, having never felt confidant with my boyfriend or the few sexual partners that followed to try anything so risqué. I suspected that everything with Iver was going to be beyond anything I'd experienced before.

Everywhere he touched me burned, adding to my heightened senses. He gently pressed against my back entrance while working the front of me. No longer able to keep my head upright, I let it drop back and let out a throaty moan. I was about to have my first orgasm, and he knew it.

"Tsk, tsk, naughty goddess, not until I say."

My head snapped back up, eyes flying open at his words. "Say what?"

He turned me, so I faced away from him and pulled my hair, drawing my head back to rest on his broad shoulder. "Not until I say 'now', may you have your orgasm, is that clear?"

"Yes," I hissed as Iver continued to play with my wet entrance.

He pulled his hand away and tightened his grip on my hair, rendering my head immobile. "Yes what, little goddess?"

Ugh, did he expect me to call him sir? Wasn't going to happen. "Yes, Iver," I gritted out.

He chuckled. "Good girl."

With my body better supported by his shoulder and chest, I closed my eyes again and let him work me like an artist creating a work of art. His strokes were masterful, and as he spoke, he whispered in a language I'd never heard before.

He reached down and tweaked my nipple with enough force to have me squeak in protest. It was aggressive; moments later, it wasn't enough. I was writhing on his lap as he worked my nipples with one hand and his fingers strummed with the other.

"Please, Iver, I can't hold on any longer."

As the word "now" fell from his lips, I exploded. My orgasm felt like it would never end. Wave after wave of sensation moved through me. He eased up for a moment and then attacked the apex of my sexual nerves and then plunged into my wet folds. I was arching to meet the thrust of his fingers and the exquisite torture of my nipples.

I knew I would be sore tomorrow, but for now, I didn't care. I felt like I was floating, flying, and falling all at once. When I finally crashed, I was boneless. Unable to stand, Iver carried me to the bed and undressed me.

Keeping my eyes open was proving challenging. Iver disappeared and came back a moment later with washcloths, one warm and wet and the other dry. He cleaned me up and dried me off. Then he pulled the covers up around me. Fearing his immediate departure, my hand shot out from under the blanket. "Don't go," I begged.

He smiled down at me. Then he undressed and climbed into bed beside me. My eyes were already closed. He pulled me onto my side and back toward him, spooning me from behind. I sighed in contentment, nestling my ass against him. Iver felt so warm and safe. Before I succumbed to sleep, I asked, "Iver, what language were you speaking?"

"Sumerian."

"Never heard of it," I mumbled and fell asleep.

Was I dreaming, or was that the enticing smell of coffee? Prying open one eye, I grabbed my phone and looked at the time. Two in the afternoon, wow, I had slept a full eight hours. It had been some time since I'd slept without nightmares waking me after a few hours of sleep. I tended to nap in the afternoons to make up for the loss of night sleep, but today I wouldn't have to.

Last night came back to me in a sudden flash. Bracing my eyes against the sunlight seeping in through the cracks in the blinds, I quickly gazed around the room. Iver was back in his chair from the previous evening, sipping coffee and watching me. Creepy much? "Good morning, may I bring you coffee in bed?"

I sat up and propped myself against the pillows. "I don't know where you found coffee, but yes, please."

Iver headed to the tiny kitchen and came back with coffee just the way I liked it, a little bit of almond creamer and lots of hot chocolate. I called them Isabelle mochas, but how could he possibly know that, and where did he get the ingredients? I was pretty sure I was out of creamer and hot chocolate.

I became very uncomfortable with how personal this was all becoming. I had meant for our time together to be one spectacular night of sex; now he was bringing me coffee in bed, not that I minded. No one had ever done that for me before. Well, my brother Jax brought me tea in bed a few times when I was sick; that was about it.

"Not to sound ungrateful, but what the hell? How do you know how I like my coffee?"

Iver chuckled. "You clearly don't remember telling me earlier when I asked you?"

I was confused. "Was I talking in my sleep?"

He gave me an indulgent grin. "Do you usually talk in your sleep?"

Control freak answering a question with a question. "I have been known to, on occasion. Now answer my question."

"Yes, I asked, and you answered. I thought you were waking up, so I hurried down to The Split Bean to get your order. I hope it's correct?"

He said the word *hope*, but his stance was his usual cocky arrogance. Wearing that all too familiar smirk, he knew perfectly well it was the way I liked it. I chose not to answer him with words, and instead drank my coffee with what I was hoping was a smile of contentment on my face.

He chuckled. "You're a little dramatic, aren't you?"

I reached behind me, grabbing hold of a pillow, and chucked it at him. Of course, he caught it. He placed it on his lap and leaned his elbows on it while watching me. Looking at him in the light of day for the first time, I could see his features better than I had in either club. Without his suit jacket on, I could see his muscles were visible beneath his rolled sleeves.

I began my eye pillaging with his gorgeous arms. The man was a god, perfect in every way. I couldn't find one damn thing about him that I didn't like, well, except the smirk that seemed painted on his face every time my eyes traveled there.

"You like what you see."

He didn't ask; he stated. "Yeah, I do, and?"

Standing up, he said, "Well, then perhaps you would like to see all of me?"

He began to strip, sliding off his expensive Fendi dress loafers—*probably custom*, I mused. Then he slid off his socks and next, his pants. He took his time, and when his pants came off, my eyes appraised his legs. They were long, with perfectly sculpted muscles, and his skin was bronze.

He slid off his shirt, and my breath hitched, and my nipples hardened. He couldn't be real; he must have had work done. I found myself gazing down at my own body and being disappointed. Until I looked at him, I thought I was pretty good looking. I had proof that many men found me attractive, but compared to his ten, I was a two.

He slid off his skin-molded boxers, and I finally got to see what he had hidden inside. His cock was as perfect as the rest of him, long enough to hit the right spot and thick enough to create friction on the way.

He strutted over to me. I put my coffee down on my side table and waited to see what his next move would be. He pulled the blanket back, reached for my ankles, and gave a gentle pull. I slid down the bed until my knees could hang off.

He placed my knees on his shoulders and bent his head down, licking the seam of my wet folds. I groaned in delight. "Yes," I chanted as his tongue danced around the bud of my excitement. Then he used it to delve deep inside of me; I felt my inner walls squeeze. At this rate, I would be orgasming in seconds.

Before I could, Iver stood up and pulled my hips to the edge of the bed. Finally, I would get to feel that magnificent cock inside of me. My god, when had I become such a wanton slut? Was it wrong to want this beautiful specimen buried deep inside of me? He grabbed a condom from his pants pocket and rolled it on.

"I'm on the pill," I stuttered.

He was already at my entrance; he didn't play as I thought he would. Instead, he buried himself to the hilt, as far inside me as he could. I contracted around his shaft and felt my orgasm pour through me. I screamed with the intensity of it.

"Good," was all he said in response to my pill comment.

He pumped into me, the friction I had imagined only moments ago coming true as I felt every inch of him inside of me. Intercourse had never been so intense. I felt another explosion of heat building deep in my core.

"Oh no, you don't, you little minx. If you come again without permission, I will stop and turn you over my knee."

"Stop."

He instantly pulled out and stood to gaze down at me.

I propped myself up on my elbows. "I want to know, right now, is this a game? Or are you the control freak I think you are and want to control every reaction my body has?"

His grin was wolfish as his gaze flicked over my naked body. "In part, this is a game, and it is also a test. I want to gauge your reaction to my words—if they affect, like I think they will. But also, I am testing to see if you can be obedient to a dominant."

Hmm, did I want this to continue? That was a good question. I read a lot of edgy romance stories and had imagined this very situation so many times. But fantasizing, and living it, were two different things. I suddenly felt the urgent need to pull the covers over my head and never get out of bed again, never face life, just drift away under this blanket. But then again, the idea of getting my fantasy, well, how many girls could say that?

"Okay."

"Okay, what, Isabelle? What do you agree to?"

"I am willing to see where this game and these tests go. We have chemistry, and I have nothing going on in my life for the next few days. I guess what I am saying, Iver, is you have six nights and seven days to play your games. In the end, I will decide if I wish to continue or walk away. Does that work for you?"

His cock, which hadn't softened during our exchange, pressed against my entrance. "Yes, Isabelle, this works for me," he said as he thrust deep inside. This time, he slowed his pace and created the most exquisite friction I've ever felt. I felt myself climbing to my orgasm, my core a confusion of sensory impulse, I could hardly tell apart all the signals.

I felt Iver lengthen inside of me and knew we were both close. A few thrusts later, "Now!" he commanded, and we both orgasmed. He rolled onto his side, taking me with him, his cock still hard inside of me. He held me tight while I snuggled my ass back into his hips. It took a long while for him to soften and finally slip from inside of me.

"That was amazing," I sighed.

"You're amazing," he responded.

I closed my eyes, and when I opened them again, it was late in the afternoon. A note was beside me on the pillow Iver had recently vacated.

Isabelle,

I will pick you up at seven for dinner. Wear something sexy, no underwear. I promise I will reward you for following my instructions. You know what happens if you don't.

Iver

Chapter 4

Iver

Leaving Isabelle asleep in her bed was difficult. I never wished to leave her side, yet I knew that the speed at which we were moving was dangerous, unless, of course, she proved to be who I thought she was. If that were the case, then not only would we continue at the breakneck speed we had created, but I would also share with her my history and the part we would play in ensuring our kind's future.

What the world had not realized yet, I still blame the Vatican for people's lack of accurate information, in that it was not only fallen angels on Earth. There were many angels on the earthly plane, and other, even stranger creatures.

The war that had ensued above was not about legalism or leadership or even good versus evil. No, the cause of the battle that resulted had been about humanity.

My father and many others happened to be collateral damage. In the fall, they were divided and left to wander the earth in search of each other or eke out a living alone. Many of the fallen did not seek each other; like my father, they stayed hidden.

Over the millenniums, most did eventually begin the path to finding other fallen. It was during that time that others, like my father, found mates and adapted into the cultures of their mates. The offspring created by these mates remained ignorant of their unique capabilities, but they carried them, nevertheless.

The fallen were celestial souls, and their offspring, with mated humans, were celestial souls sequestered in human bodies. Unlike my father, who was a full angel who had fallen, these offspring of the fallen had immortality only, unless other gifts were bestowed upon them by birthright of the other parent.

To my knowledge, none had any powers beyond immortality. But the fallen had chosen dominant mates, like my father with Freya. The coupling of a god and an angel had provided me with untold power.

The kicker was unless the fallen shared their identity and awoke immortality in their children, they died a mortal death. I don't understand the reasoning behind allowing an immortal to die. Through much discussion with my father on the matter, we both believed it was fear driving their decision, and unwanted attention by the fallen that were far from having positive intentions toward the remaining fallen and humanity.

Despite my age, I have never encountered an immortal offspring with exceptional powers, except one, the only female ruler to have ever sat on the throne of Canaan. Her fallen name was Ariella and her name meant lioness; ironically, she had stayed hidden until she started a movement in her kingdom around four thousand years ago, the Mistress of the lionesses.

Ariella had mated with a roman god, Apollo, and retained

the ability to pass on her birthright to her offspring directly, with no activation required.

Having a father who was God's scribe, had its advantages. According to my father, every thousand years or so, Ariella passed on her special powers to a female offspring. Ariella gave birth in 1200 BC to Arin, in 200 BC to Alwain and 1200AD to Aster. The latest one would now be twenty years old, born in 2000AD, and I believed that girl to be Isabelle, born Ariel.

Ariella's family traveled from Canaan to Egypt to Africa to Spain to Scotland and, finally, the past hundred years, into America. My father said they were unique to the fallen but had never shared how. During her early time on Earth, Ariella had thought it prudent to allow her family to disperse, meaning she felt it wise to keep their lineage a secret.

Michael, God's prince, the top of the heavenly host, found us in Los Angeles. He shared with Enoch the obliteration of Ariella's line, except for the youngest, Ariel. All three of her daughters and herself were killed in different locations at the same time, by hellfire; her descendants not sired directly by her, and Apollo, were gunned down or killed in a way to look like suicide or accidents.

We were shocked; my father wasn't privy to information that could kill immortals, except other immortals. For hellfire to be on Earth, Michael said, there was someone who knew of its power and had found a way to use it. If Ariel died, the fallen would go extinct, their light in the world extinguished forever.

Michael charged me with finding Ariella's most recent descendant, Ariel, and ensuring two things: one, that she was protected, and two, that she fall in love and mate with the most potent celestial being on Earth, me.

Chapter 5

Isabelle

I put the note down and had naughty thoughts, imagining myself precariously perched over Iver's lap. I wondered if a G-string counted as underwear. My stomach rumbled, time to get up. Puttering to the kitchen, I opened my fridge and groaned.

Nothing but a few old take out containers, ugh. I threw on my jeans and a t-shirt and ran down three flights of stairs and out the front door, across the street to my favorite bagel place. The owners, Tino and his wife, Rea, treated me like family. They must have seen me because they were already toasting a lox and cream cheese bagel and frothing a latte.

"Ciao, Tino, Rea, how did you know?"

"Isabelle, you should know by now that we always know when you have a craving, and it is usually about this time." I glanced up at the clock. Sure enough, it was 4:30, my usual timing. I grinned, pulling out a twenty from my pocket.

"No, Bella, we will not take your money." I thanked them and headed to the door.

"Isabelle," Rea called as I opened the door. "I wish you'd been here this morning. The most gorgeous man I've ever seen came in and ordered a black coffee and your favorite almond milk hot chocolate mocha."

I turned, trying to hide the blush that suddenly spread across my cheeks.

Thankfully, Tino spoke up. "Most gorgeous man, what about me, eh?" Tino began to waltz toward his wife. They were adorable, and it was Rea who ended up with the blush. Saved by Tino, I waved and headed out the door.

Back in my tiny apartment, I sat back with my coffee and bagel. I was starving, demolishing the bagel in under a minute. As I took my first sip from my coffee, my phone rang. I glanced down at my cell to see if it was Iver. *Jax* flashed on my screen. I rolled my eyes; my first instinct was to ignore the call.

"Yo," I answered.

"Isabelle, it's your brother, Jax."

I laughed. "Bro, what century are you living in? I know it's you."

Dead silence, my brother hated being teased. Jax had zero sense of humor. We didn't get along in the slightest, and he only called when he wanted to see me. A sense of duty, no doubt, to make sure I was still alive.

"You're so insolent, Isabelle."

My hackles rose. "And you are an obnoxious prick, but I'm not complaining, and neither should you."

"I think you should come home, young lady, and take a trip over my knee."

"Jax. You're pissing me off. Is that why you called? If so, I'm hanging up now."

"No, wait, Isabelle, sorry, don't hang up. I'm calling because I'm in your neck of the woods tomorrow, and I wanted to know if you had time for lunch."

I didn't want to see him; we were like oil and water. Jax

always tried to control me, how I dressed, and what I said, what I did for a living. I purposely did things to show my distaste. It's hard, though, when you have two older brothers and no parents. They tag-teamed, checking in on me, their annoying sister. I guess Jax lost the coin toss this time around.

"Yah, sure, but I pick the place."

I could feel him rolling his eyes. "Fine," he huffed, "where?"

"I'll text you the name and address. See you tomorrow." I hung up the phone and quickly texted him the address for the Witch's Brew. I laughed, wishing I could see his face when he read my text. Jax hated the all-vegan café, with its crystals hanging everywhere. The truth was I only went there when Jax called a family luncheon. I wasn't a fan of it, either, but I knew he hated it, and I wanted to piss him off.

I was in a grumpy mood and no longer looked forward to my latte. I dumped it in the sink and headed to my closet. What to wear for Mr. Sexy? Would he be too embarrassed to be seen in public with me and take me to a little out of the way place? Or would he go all out and take me to one of those exclusive restaurants on Madison Park Ave?

Decisions, I did have one dress; it was clingy but not sleazy, mid-thigh length and the color matched my eyes, emerald green, my best feature. I was unusually pale, more so since our band had gotten regular gigs. I was more vampire looking than anything, my dark hair adding to that vampiric quality.

I tried on my thigh-high black boots; now I looked sleazy and perfect for a club outing. But this was dinner, with a wealthy, attractive, dominant male. I reached into the back of my closet and found some black Italian pumps. They were gorgeous, and I'd found them in a barely worn clothing and accessories store in Soho village, of all places.

I owned very little jewelry, but I did own one priceless piece passed down from my mother and through the female line in my family. It was a beautiful moonstone with two diamonds hovering around it like stars. The stone itself was relatively large and would have been overwhelming on a shorter woman. As I was 5'7", I could pull it off.

I placed everything at the foot of my rumpled bed and headed into the shower. I decided to shave all my bits, so I was as smooth as a baby down there. He didn't request that I shave my nether region, but I had a feeling he would be pleased if I did so. With no undies, I would be open and vulnerable.

Vulnerable, that should turn on a man like Iver, and why not turn him on? Our date may be the only ever high-end date, and I may as well enjoy it.

I soaked in my half tub until the water got cold. After toweling off, I did my hair and then my make-up. I usually did dark make up when I played, lots of heavy eyeliner. When I wasn't playing, I didn't wear any. I liked letting my skin breathe.

I scrolled through Pinterest and found a few looks that would work for me that were more classic. I raided my makeup drawer, pulling out enough make up for a herd of models. I mimicked a classical look, with light eyeliner and smoky eyes and light pink-tinged gloss, to highlight my natural lip color instead of disguising it.

Standing back, angling my face in different directions in the mirror, I decided I liked the finished product. It was very different than my usual look. I used makeup like many women did, as armor. To change one's armor or wear less when going into battle was a strange sensation. But I was taking a leap of faith with this date, so I pulled out all the stops.

I decided I kind of liked the different look I'd created. Next was my hair, which took only ten minutes; my hair is short. It was styled in a pixie cut, like the character Alice, from *Twilight*. My hair was thick, and I found it way easier to manage at a shorter length, and with my heart-shaped face, my short locks showed me off better.

I had a little extra time, so I sat and went through my emails and checked my Instagram page, the band's Instagram page, I didn't have one of my own. I hated social media but offered to do our postings for the group. It was only fair as Marshall was our sound expert and put in extra hours with that, and Steve booked our gigs. Other than the social media posts, there was not a lot else I did to support the band.

Finished with Instagram, it was time to get dressed. I watched myself in my full-length mirror that hung on the back of my closet door. I put on a lacy bra with a matching thong, thought better of it and instead stuffed the thong into my purse. It was my choice, after all. I could opt to listen to his request, or I could be a brat and do whatever I wanted.

Next, I put on the dress and the pumps and finally the moonstone and then gazed at the finished product. Damn, I looked hot. I'd do me, I laughed at my image. I took a few selfies just to remind myself I cleaned up well and headed down the stairs. I'd been waiting two minutes when the hairs on the back on my neck stood.

It was a familiar sensation, having the hair on my neck stand on end. Maybe Iver was playing a game and had already arrived and was spying on me? I looked across the street, scanning the doorways for predators. I didn't see anyone, but I couldn't shake the feeling that someone was watching me.

I was about to walk to the end of the block when I heard a rumble. I looked in the direction of the rumbling. The hottest car I'd ever seen was heading my way, a cobalt blue Shelby Cobra, original 427 with racing stripes. Wow, it was hotter moving than it was the one time I'd seen one parked. My jaw must have hit the cement when Iver pulled up beside me with a big grin on his face.

He hopped out and then stopped and appraised me from toe to head. I felt myself blushing and hoped he couldn't see my pink cheeks in the darkness of the night.

"Wow, I'm honored you put so much effort into dressing for me. You look stunning, drop-dead gorgeous, Isabelle." He opened the passenger door for me and helped me sink into my seat.

"This is a sweet ride, Iver," I said when he was back in the driver's seat. I had been in love with the make and model of this Cobra since my father had taken me to a car show. My father had asked the owner if he could take a picture of me inside his car. The man had allowed it, and I still had that picture somewhere.

I stroked the interior of the car lovingly.

"Would you like to drive it after dinner?"

"Really?" A smile lit my face. "That would be fantastic, thank you."

He smirked. "You are welcome, Isabelle, or do you prefer Issy?"

There was something in the way he said Issy that hit a trigger deep in my subconscious. A series of images of me trying to hide from Robert Voss played in quick succession. I was unable to control my reaction, and one traitorous tear slid down my cheek.

"Please, don't ever call me Issy. I absolutely hate it. Isabelle is fine, or Bella is also fine. Issy belongs to a little girl, and I am not that person."

He didn't pry, kudos to him. I managed to let go of the melancholy moment and move on, again running my hand over the leather of the Cobra and appreciating the work of art that was this car.

I knew we were traveling west but had no idea where exactly he was taking me. Fifteen minutes later, Iver pulled up in front of an elegantly treed parking space. Helping me out of the vehicle was a valet dressed in a tux. "Welcome to Chez Henri," he said with a French accent.

I looked around excitedly. I knew the place cost a fortune.

I'd heard through the online rumor mill that a dining experience here was an enjoyable, three-hour minimum affair. It was a dining experience that was unparalleled.

Despite my promise to myself to not be overly impressed by his wealth, I squealed with delight.

He laughed. "I'm glad you approve, Bella."

The restaurant was not visible from where we stood. I looked questioningly at Iver. He smiled, and taking my arm and placing it through his, we headed toward a recessed enclosure. As we stepped through a gate and onto a red carpet, I spotted a small forest ahead. It must be shrouding the restaurant, I surmised, and a twenty-foot privacy wall. Wait, what? How was that possible in the middle of the city?

The wonder must have shown on my face. "Pictures are forbidden here. If you try to take one, you would be required to delete it upon entry into the restaurant. That is why you never see this part on social media. Can you imagine the uproar it would stir?"

I nodded in agreement. "I guess you have foreknowledge of the main entrance, or do we just keep following the red carpet?"

Iver smiled, and the twinkle lights that lit up the small forest illuminated his face. He looked genuinely pleased with himself, control freak, just loved keeping me on my toes.

"The entrance is unique; watch as we get closer, the forest seems to part."

He was right; I was fascinated. From the street, a person would have no idea what was back here. Even once through the gate, I could see a small forest but nothing else. But as we followed the red carpet, it was like an optical illusion. What was hidden from the street and the gate suddenly came into focus.

I was speechless as I stood staring up at the restaurant, housed in a glass dome and filled with exotic plants, a waterfall that deposited into a stream that ran throughout, and birds. "Wow, just wow, Iver, I don't know what to say. My senses feel like they just went on vacation to some exotic land."

He chuckled as he guided me up the steps. At the door, we were greeted. "Mr. Eriskay, Ms. Ackels, good evening." Our host bowed and then escorted us to the very back and then some. We passed diners and some pretty famous ones at that. I spotted the who's who in musicians, politicians, actors, activists.

The restaurant held fifty or so tables, and all were spread out and enclosed by flora, giving the feeling that one was dining in the jungle, and the only things missing were the wild animals and ants.

We passed all of the diners, making our way to the back of the restaurant and an enclosed private dining room that looked to be a miniature of the larger dining area. The lighting came from twinkle lights entwined in the trees and bushes and a few antique wrought iron chandeliers. On our table were floating candles in the shapes of exotic flowers.

I knew my eyes were huge, taking in our surroundings and looking like the newbie I was, but I couldn't help it. Our host was about to pull out my chair, but Iver waved him off and did it instead. He stroked my neck before moving to his chair.

"This place must cost a fortune."

"It does," Iver responded. "I already offered to stay and do the dishes."

I laughed. "Okay smart guy, this is impressive, but if you think I'm going to be your sex slave because you can afford nice dinners, you are wrong, I won't sell my soul to the devil, not even one as handsome as you."

"Darn, and here I was about to offer you a million dollars for the rest of your life. That does seem rather cheap, to buy such a bold and beautiful woman. How about a billion?" he deadpanned.

"Very funny, ha, ha. No amount would suffice. But if I fell

in love with the perfect man who treated me well, it may be possible."

"Touché, lovely lady."

A bottle of champagne was sitting in an ice bucket beside our table. Iver popped the cork and poured us each a glass.

"To falling in love," he said as he held up his glass for a toast.

"Sure, I'll toast to the possibility."

Iver laughed as our glasses made the most beautiful resonating *ching* sound. Have to love expensive crystal.

Chapter 6

Iver

Watching Isabelle was better entertainment than a movie. Her expressions were pure; she wore her heart on her sleeve. I wondered if that was one of the reasons why her band was so well received, the hot female drummer who looked like she was having a love affair with her instrument when she played.

When she was off stage, she was reserved, not cold, but she was good at protecting herself. The car incident was surprising. Something had happened to her, and from her brief declaration regarding her name, I gathered it had happened young.

Whoever was responsible for the tear that slid down her face was going to pay. Who would want to hurt such an enchanting creature? Stupid question, many people wanted to make other people hurt because they could, and I hoped it was something as simple as that and not some fallen monster who had figured out what she was.

The fallen were different, and we could tell when others of our kind were near. We smelled different, each unique, and

Isabelle smelled like cinnamon and cream. To other immortals, she would be hard to ignore.

Even the fallen had weaknesses, and not all were like me, dedicated to serving the planet we lived on in the best way possible. No one but my father and Michael knew about my work or my assignment to help Ariella's last daughter.

To any immortal, Isabelle would smell like candy. She would be anyone's weakness; I could see them not wanting to let her go. I didn't want to let her go and fervently hoped she was Ariel, Ariella's youngest and last descendant, because the idea of spending the next thousand years or longer with Isabelle was my idea of paradise.

All through our dinner, she moaned, commented and made noises of approval with each bite. With each sound, my cock would stand at attention. Her moans were not the only sounds, although those alone would have been enough to make me hard. She closed her eyes, and she licked her lips. When dessert arrived, Isabelle looked like a woman who'd been engaging in sex all evening instead of eating.

My god, the woman was sexy beyond anything. I fervently sent a prayer to Michael, to let her be the one. Of course, there was a simple way to find out. I could try activating her immortality; only a fallen or an angel could do that for another.

But first, I had six days to get her to trust me, to believe the story I would share with her, and get to know her family. There were secrets in her lineage that I could uncover by tracing backward. Learning family history would be dependent on her living relatives' ancestral knowledge.

We'd finished dessert. "Well, Isabelle, was it the best you've ever had?" I smirked at the double entendre. She blushed. We'd had a different wine pairing with each dish. Driving the Cobra would have to wait until the next day. If pulled over, she would score high on a Breathalyzer test.

"I'm not entirely sure," she said, smacking her lips. "I think

I need another taste to determine if I've truly experienced the best I've ever had. I'm pretty sure we could find out in that copping of bushes over there. What do you say?"

"I like your minx side. I think she is Bella," I said in a teasing tone. She was wearing a come-hither look, desire evident by her dilated pupils. My cock, which had felt like a springboard all night, hardening and softening, was in dire need of sinking into her hot entrance.

I went over to the door and flipped over a sign that was hanging on the doorknob, turned the lock and stalked back. Leaning down, my face only inches from hers, I said, "If you want to play with me, Bella, you must do as you're told, understand?"

Her face went through a myriad of expressions, the final one, acceptance. But of course, she added in her condition. "You will honor our agreement if I say stop?"

"Of course, I will. What do you take me for, a monster?"

I was kidding, but her eyes grew serious. "No, Iver, I've met monsters, and you're not one of those. But I'm not sure what you are or who you truly are. I feel as if we are just playing, and as entertaining as that is, I would like to know the truth about why you found me in the club, why you sent me drinks every night, why you invited my band to Raphe's friend's club. And most of all, why me?"

Her words were sage for someone so young. But the force behind them caught me by surprise. She was powerful and utterly unaware of it. If she were Ariel, I would help her develop her gifts, her immortal voice being one of them.

The instant she delivered her empowered words, a whole new level of attraction sprung up, and I wanted her, badly. I needed to bond and feel the power that existed just below the surface. Immortals were a lusty group and coupling between the souls was euphoric.

I stood back and held out my hand to her. Taking it, I drew

her in tight, claiming her mouth with mine. She opened to me and allowed my tongue to delve into her sweetness. Her taste, a blend of coffee, champagne and chocolate, combined with her natural scent, drove in me such a deep desire to taste her nectar.

I drew her over to a giant planter and sat her on the edge. She leaned back against the bamboo the stand housed. I lifted her dress and bent down, licking her seam. She moaned out loud and gently thrust toward my mouth. I alternated between licking her hardening bud and delving into her dripping entrance. I continued my sensual assault, feeling the electric current from my tongue to her core.

"Iver," she moaned. "Please, I need to let go, please."

"Because you asked so nicely, you may."

Bella was like a dam; upon release, her essence poured out of her and onto my tongue. As I lapped up her juices, I felt like I was absorbing a piece of who she was, a piece of the immortality I was sure she possessed. I wondered if she were more, as I had been alive for several millennia and never had I felt what I did right then with her.

I plunged two fingers deep inside and alternated between pressing them in and pinching her little sensitive nub. She squealed as she came on my fingers and tongue. She was almost panting and crying at the same time with the intensity of her release. I could no longer hold back, my desire to be inside of her so primal. I undid my zipper, barely getting the condom rolled down, before slamming into her molten core.

Bella was like a crazed woman with an insane itch, bucking as hard as she could. I reached down, grabbing her ass, and picked her up and then pressed her down onto my cock, thrusting deep inside of her, splitting her wider, claiming her. Her multiple orgasms continued to rip through her body, and finally, I let go, both of us climaxing at the same time.

I stumbled back onto a chair with her still on top of me.

She leaned into my chest, her panting breath beginning to slow down. When she was able to move, I stood her up and pulled her dress down. "We need to get out of here and get cleaned up."

I unlocked the door, turning the sign around. Our waiter entered less than a minute later. "Sir?" he asked.

"The bill and my car, to the back exit, please."

"Yes, sir, I assumed you would be ready; the car is out back, and your bill applied to your account."

Thank you, please add twenty percent in addition to the regular gratuity."

The waiter smiled for the first time that evening. "Yes, sir, and thank you, sir."

I nodded and then escorted Isabelle out the back and into the waiting vehicle. "You can drive tomorrow, my love. You've had too much alcohol, and you need to rest, yes?"

She nodded and closed her eyes, falling instantly asleep.

Chapter 7

Jax

My excuse for seeing my sister would be new offices. She would want a reason; she always did. During a phone call with our brother, Finn, he'd let slip that her band had wrapped up their current gig, and she would be off for a week. A perfect time to check in on her, as she couldn't use a gig as an excuse not to see me.

My younger brother, Finn, is friends with Marshall, Isabelle's bass player. Both good looking geeks met at a graphics convention. Marshall was looking for a group to join, so Finn introduced him to Steve and Issy, as their bass player had just quit, and they were looking for a replacement. One could say that it was a fortuitous meeting.

Not me, I didn't believe in that new age energy crap that so many people swallowed without questioning. Karma? Really? The universe's will or path? Really? What a lot of hooey. I believed in logic and good old-fashioned work ethic. Some-times things worked out, and sometimes they didn't, simple facts.

My sister had a work ethic, but beyond that, we didn't see eye to eye on anything. In my opinion, Issy was a loose cannon, and at twenty years old, I had no say over her life. She moved into mid-town central three years ago. Back then, Finn, at twenty-one, was living in the same neighborhood.

She had just finished high school, and all she wanted to do was play drums. Who was I to stop her? Steve and Isabelle had been friends in their senior year; they'd met in band. As he, too, was moving to the city, I knew if I tried to keep her in Jersey, she would just run away, so I cut the ties and signed off on her flying the coop.

Those first two years, Finn kept his eye on her, which was better for Issy than being around me, as those two got on better than she and I. The two of them had lunch dates a few times per month, and being Marshall and Finn were friends, he went out to some of the gigs as well.

I kept my distance from Issy, and my checking in was mainly by telephone, except for birthdays and Christmas. But now, with Finn gone from the neighborhood, we took turns officially checking in on her. I know she wasn't looking forward to meeting me for lunch. Heck, I wasn't, either, but she was my sister, and her health and safety were important to me.

The hour and a half drive time to Manhattan allowed me to play soothing music and think on how to keep my cool over lunch. I knew she would press my buttons; she always did. She also knew I would lose it and then storm out of wherever we were having lunch. I chuckled; maybe she was smarter than I realized.

If I were she, I'd be doing the same thing in the hopes of getting out of an obligation early. My sister was a rare jewel as a child. I'd loved her fiercely and had spoiled her rotten. Life back then had been peaceful and loving until she hit age eleven.

She became a nightmare. Isabelle said she hated Brooklyn,

so I moved us to Jersey, a block from the beach and for a while, that seemed to appease her. She never was a star in school, but her grades dropped even more in high school.

She started hanging with the artsy, gothic crowd and became opinionated, aggressive and was prone to fighting. Grade eight through ten, I was called to her principal's office. Often, she wasn't to blame, and I did my best to deter her from getting in over her head in potentially socially explosive situations.

I missed the cute little girl with the big green eyes. I don't know what caused such a radical shift in her behavior, and whenever I tried talking to her about it, she would close up. I parked in front of Witch's Brew, home to organic, vegan every-thing. She wasn't a vegan; she wasn't even a vegetarian.

I think she secretly enjoyed torturing me; the restaurant slash gift shop sold crystals and amulets and all kinds of crap. Having lunch here was a trigger in itself, trying to talk to her without losing my shit would be next to impossible.

Again, I wondered if that had been her plan from the beginning. I was about to get out of my car when a text came in from Issy.

Issy: *Meet me at Craft 43rd E.19. Bringing a friend.*
   Me: *Okay, see you in a few.*

She was bringing a friend. I wondered if it was Steve or Marshall, but she would have said so, I was sure of it. So, who was this *friend?* I didn't think Issy had any friends outside of the band, and definitely not anyone she'd want me to meet. I arrived and handed my keys to the valet. Craft was the most expensive restaurant we'd ever met in. I began to wonder if the *friend* she was bringing with her was wealthy.

I was walking up the steps when I heard a rumble. Glancing around, I saw a rare sports car making all the noise. The mint condition Cobra pulled up and parked. Ha. I laughed. Issy would be so jealous she missed this. I knew it was her favorite car. I waited to see an old man exit the vehicle as this was a reliving your youth kind of car that cost a small fortune.

Instead, a gorgeous guy in his mid-late twenties got out of the passenger seat and opened the driver's door. Reaching his hand in, she stepped out. My jaw almost hit the pavement. It was my sister, driving a half a million-dollar car with a gorgeous, obviously rich guy groveling at her feet. What kind of witchcraft was this?

After helping her out, the man pulled her in for a deep kiss that lasted longer than was considered proper in public. She pushed him away with a giggle and straightened her skirt. I looked at her from head to toe; she was outfitted to the nines and looked like a model. Now I knew aliens had abducted the real Issy.

I didn't know if I should go into Craft and get a table, pretending I didn't see anything, or act like her prudish older brother and set the tone for our lunch, or plaster a smile on my face and pretend this was all normal. In the end, I chose option three. Issy waved, and I waited for her and her *friend*, with a smile plastered on my face.

When she and the hot guy had caught up, she air-kissed me on both cheeks. I was getting concerned; she had never done that before in her life.

"Hi, Jax, meet Iver. Iver, this is Jax, my oldest brother."

"Hello, Jax," Iver said, reaching out his hand and taking mine in a firm grip. I was a big guy, muscular from hours at the gym and sports on the weekends, but he was buffer, and even though I considered myself passably good looking, this guy was just plain hot. Sexy GQ meets Viking warrior. No wonder Issy was acting differently. She probably was suffering from an over-abundance of pink endorphins, making her stupid.

"Hope you don't mind me tagging along, Jax, I insisted on meeting you."

A red flag. Iver oozed dominance. I wondered if he looked at my sister as a challenge. Issy didn't have a submissive bone in her body. "Really? Well, here I am. Should we go inside and get better acquainted?"

I wasn't acting cold, but I wasn't friendly, either. I could see Issy's reaction to my attitude, and I knew she wanted to say something unkind. He must have picked up on it, too, as he grabbed her hand and raised it to his lips.

"Come, my fair maiden. I need to feed you; let us get inside. I have a reservation, but the place does get busy." With that, he opened the door and waited for us both to pass through before bringing up the rear.

A host greeted us and then bowed to Iver. "Mr. Eriskay, nice to see you back, sir; your table is ready."

I looked at Issy; she smiled back at me as if she hadn't a care in the world. She was such a brat. I hung back a bit, following our party to a private dining room. Every woman's head in the place turned as Iver walked by. Figures, total play-boy. I didn't need to get to know this guy. He would be out of the picture in a few days. Issy didn't like show-offs.

Once we were seated, our waiter poured sparkling water into Bormioli rock bar glasses. He withdrew, leaving us to make our menu selections.

"Well, Isabelle, this is a far cry from the Witch's Brew, where you normally make me suffer."

She laughed, outright laughed. "I thought you would appreciate the upgrade, brother. Besides, I didn't feel right about parking the Cobra outside the vegan restaurant, with the type of clientele that it draws. Iver's car may have ended up with a paint job. I heard that those nuts who used to throw red paint on fur coats are now throwing it on anything that resembles wealth."

"That's a thing? New York is crazy; maybe I won't open offices here after all."

Iver zeroed in on me. "What building were you looking at?"

Shit, I didn't do my research because I knew Issy would never have asked me that, as she couldn't have cared less. I thought about recent acquisitions that had been on the market recently. "The water street corridor; there are many up for grabs right now," I answered. That was general enough to not back me into a corner I couldn't dig myself out.

"That's fantastic. I own several offices in those buildings, and if you allowed, I would love to clear my calendar for the rest of the day and take you on a personal tour."

Damn him, calling me on my bluff. His eyes glittered with amusement. He knew I was full of shit. I didn't know what I wanted to do more, punch the guy, or take him up on his offer. At the very least, it would be a chance to see the inner workings of the city culture.

"I don't want you to have to take time away from your busy schedule for me."

Thinking the conversation would end there, I almost choked on my water when he said, "My pleasure, Jax. My little minx here, Bella, has an afternoon at the spa, getting those drummer's knots worked out. In fact, why don't you be my guest in the city tonight and come out for dinner with Isabelle and me? That would be fun, wouldn't it, my love?"

Isabelle, who had remained silent during our exchange, gazed into his eyes and said with a totally straight face, "Yes, my love, that would be fun."

"Wonderful!" He clapped his hands. The waiter must have heard as he came scurrying over to the table to take our order. It was amusing and sobering. Whoever this guy was, he outranked and outclassed me by a landslide. And suddenly, it was all clear. Isabelle wanted this to play out this way. She wanted me humbled and at her mercy for a change.

When our wine arrived, Iver poured, and I held up my hand. "A toast."

Iver smiled in encouragement; the man was arrogant.

"To my sister, a fine strategist."

Iver's eyes glinted, and Issy smirked. Now she knew that I knew her game. Ha, at least I had that satisfaction.

Chapter 8

Isabelle

I woke up in complete darkness, rubbing my eyes as I sat up. I gazed around the space, allowing my eyes time to adjust. Last night came back to me in a flood of memories and riding on the sensations.

Just thinking about the intensity of our sex was making me tingly all over. I'd never experienced anything so intense. Everything with Iver felt primal, and the man was a god in the sack. I sighed in contentment until my bladder told me it was time to pee.

Getting up, I headed toward the door on the opposite wall. I took note of the deep plush of the carpet I treaded on. It felt expensive. The bathroom was like a high-end hotel, with vases of flowers and everything pristine. Men's bathrooms were never immaculate. I wish they were, but I knew from experience growing up with two brothers that men were absolute pigs.

When I came out of the bathroom, the blinds were open to a stunning view of the Manhattan skyline. A naked Iver was on the bed with two steaming cups of coffee in his hands. "Well, you certainly know how to greet a woman." I sashayed over to the bed and grabbed a cup.

"How was your sleep, Bella?"

"Very, very good. And I don't normally sleep well, three maybe four hours, and then I wake up." Now I was curious to know the time. I had something at noon, what was it? Right, Jax.

"Shit, what time is it?"

"Relax, it's only 8:30, but you slept a long time; you fell asleep in the car around eleven last night."

I sighed and sat back, hooding my eyes, moving my focus to the perfect coffee I was sipping. But I guess my face must have betrayed me.

"Isabelle, is the coffee wrong? Why are you frowning?"

I laughed. "Oh, if only it were the coffee. No, Iver, the coffee is perfect. I have my annual lunch date with my brother, Jax, today at noon, and I don't want to go."

He seemed to consider my words. "May I ask why?" I opened my eyes, fully taking him in. Should I tell him? How much could I safely reveal regarding my relationship with my estranged brother?

"We don't get along." I decided, the less, the better.

Merriment shone in Iver's eyes. "That's it, you don't get along? Says every girl out there about their older brother."

I chuckled. "Okay, we don't like each other and haven't for a long time. Does that answer your question?"

He took my mug and placed on the nightstand and then pressed me back into the pillows. Gathering my wrists in his hand, he leaned down and took my nipple in his mouth. He bit down, and I felt a zing shoot from my nipple to my sex.

"You fight dirty," I panted.

His tongue was doing some dirty dancing on my nipple, swirling all kinds of sensations. Then he moved to the other and bit down, causing another wave of electricity to run from the tip of my nipple to my sex. I began to undulate beneath him, craving him inside of me.

"You have no idea," he commented as he blew on my nipple. I felt it pebble under his breath. He nudged my legs apart with his knee and planted the tip of his hard length at my entrance. I thrust my hips in response, but he didn't move farther in. I tried bucking closer. His hand around my wrists was like an iron band, holding me in place.

"Grrr, Iver," I growled. "What the hell? Fuck me already. Or get off me; you're pissing me off."

That got his attention. His eyes glittered dangerously. "Am I pissing you off?"

"Yes, you ruined the moment. Get off me; I need to have a shower and go home."

That was too demanding for Iver the Dom. He let go, sat down, and pulled me over his lap in one fell swoop. "I'm sorry to hear that you are not interested in having hours of pleasure, Isabelle. Regardless, I don't appreciate your tone or your demands." He slammed his hand down on my upturned backside.

"Ouch. Stop it."

He smacked his hand down several more times, alternating between each cheek. "Are you using your safe word, Isabelle, and ending our time together prematurely? Or are you just being a baby? You can't get hurt from a spanking. I promise what I do, you won't feel tomorrow, and if we stop now, you won't receive the aftercare. I don't think you want to miss out on that."

There was aftercare? What the hell was that? While I suffered from indecision, the spanking he was delivering was having a profound effect on me. The heat from my ass was penetrating to my core, returning my hunger for intercourse.

Instead of using a safe word, I arched my back, accommodating his large hand on my backside.

He began to spank the underside of my cheeks.

"Ouch, ouch, ouch, I don't like that spot; go back to the other spot," I blurted.

He laughed and hit my sit spots harder. "No demands, young lady, take your punishment like a good girl."

Before I could spit out some nasty words that would no doubt get me into even deeper trouble, Iver plunged a finger inside my molten womb.

"Oh, oh, yes, please," I begged.

Iver's spanking rhythm changed, becoming lighter and quicker, while his other hand alternated between my hardening nub and plunging into my soaking core. I was climbing to my first orgasm, and he knew it.

"Not yet, my little sex goddess." He lifted me off his lap like I weighed nothing, and standing up, he pulled me to the edge of the bed and had me get on my hands and knees. I wondered what my ass looked like all heated up, with my glistening entrance exposed. I should have been horrified, but instead, I felt sexy.

In one thrust, Iver entered me, his hands reaching under me and tweaking both nipples, and that was it. I shattered, my orgasm taking me to new heights, and when I crashed, I felt myself falling and wondered briefly if the bed was moving.

He slapped my ass with one hand while his other gripped my nipples. Usually, the force would have been way too much, but I was on fire and had an itch that needed scratching. "Oh, god, yes," I groaned. "Yes, yes." I was turning into a slut, but I couldn't help myself. I wanted to cry and scream and shout to the rooftops; my body was an electric impulse that was building. Just when I thought I couldn't take it anymore, he changed the angle, and I screamed my release. I knew Iver was emptying into the condom and I hoped it would hold up against the endless hot jets spilling into it. I couldn't feel anything concrete beneath me. I was hovering on a cloud of bliss when Iver pulled out and dropping on the bed, pulling me against his front for a snuggle. I was landed and back connected with Earth.

"Okay little minx, can you tell me now, what is the deal with you and your brother?"

I wanted to. I wanted to tell Iver everything, to unload for the first time and share the burden with another, but was Iver the right person?

He must have sensed my struggle. "Isabelle, I promise you that I will keep your secret and help you in any way I can if you require any of me. If nothing else, maybe I could be your confidant, and you could unburden yourself. I sense the weight you are carrying in regard to your brother is a heavy one."

I didn't know if it was his words or the kindness and sincerity in his tone, but I started to cry. Something I never did, I fought instead of crying. Iver pulled me closer, encircling me in his warmth and strength, allowing me to feel safe in a way I never thought possible.

"I-I'm not sure where to begin. I-I mean, we got along okay when I was little. Jax adored me, and I looked up to him. Sometime around age eleven, he became a little distant, and he stopped spending time with me. Until then, he'd take me for ice cream; we had like a sibling date once a week. It was fun, and we would talk about school. Well, I would; he was graduated and working by then. I developed early; I didn't look much different than I do now. Jax and Finn's friends began to notice me, and I know it pissed Jax off. I am ashamed to say that I outright flirted with Jax's buddies to get back at him for ignoring me. Jax's friends thought the flirting cute. Jax, not so much. I think we would have killed each other if not for Finn. Finn was, and still is, a filter between Jax and me. I was grateful to Finn for his intervention, although I rarely showed it. I was angry all the time."

I felt Iver's arm tighten on me, his body hardening behind me in anticipation of the rest of my story. He had good instincts, for what I was going to share would either push him away from me in disgust or pull us even closer together.

"As I approached age twelve, I wanted out of Jax's clutches. He watched me like a hawk, and if I ever stepped out of line, he was nasty. I spent as much time as I could with my girl-friends, and that's when I started playing drums. Drums were a great way to relieve my stress. I find it fills me up artistically and gives me a physical discharge, so I don't implode. Anyway, I was in the garage practicing my drums one day. Neither Jax nor Finn was home, when one of Jax's buddies walked in the garage. I didn't like this particular friend; he was always leering at me, and it wasn't the fun flirty stuff that I did with Jax's other friends. This guy gave off bad vibes."

I began shaking. Why was it so freakin' hard to share what had happened? I was disgusted and ashamed and many other things, that's why. It was my secret and one I'd never shared with another person. Iver turned me around so he could look into my eyes. His were a mix of love and anger. I think he knew what I was going to say, but he waited patiently, encouraging me silently to continue.

I blew out a breath and steadied myself. "I don't want to describe the details. I will give you the gist of things, and if you ask questions, I will answer yes or no. I am having a tough time saying this out loud, as I've never spoken of it, ever."

"I understand, Isabelle, it's okay. You are okay, and what-ever you don't want to share is fine with me. You are so brave; just keep going."

"Okay, well, He came over to the drum set and asked me to part my legs wider. I was wearing shorts. I told him to go fuck himself. And he said, 'Why would I do that, when I have such sweet meat right here in front of me?' The long and short of it is he attacked me, and I did my best to fight him off. In the process, I managed to sustain considerable bruising. He punched me and kicked me into submission, and then he raped me."

I could tell Iver was straining to hold back his rage. Finally, he said, "And your brothers don't know?"

"No, I never told anyone."

"Didn't they wonder what happened to you?

"Yes, but I told them I got jumped by some high school kids on my way home from school, and I never saw them coming."

"Did you go to the hospital?"

"Yes, but they only checked to make sure I hadn't broken any bones, and thankfully nothing was."

"How have you been dealing with the trauma all these years?"

I sighed and gazed into his beautiful eyes. "I don't, Iver, that is why I have nightmares and don't sleep. Last night was probably the first time since then that I've slept an entire night." I grinned. "So thank you for that; it was truly a gift, better than any restaurant."

He smiled. "I will give you the world if you let me, Isabelle."

Attempting to lighten the mood, I answered, "Let's just get through the next few days first. I gotta make sure you're all that you appear to be."

Iver leaned up on one forearm. He was hatching a plan; I could tell by the glint in his eyes. "Isabelle, may I make a suggestion regarding today?"

I rolled onto my back. "Sure, anything, now that you know why it's so hard for me to see my brother. When we moved, at my insistence, I hoped things would get better. But they didn't. Instead, Finn and I grew closer, and then he met Marshall at a

Comicon or graphics thing, I don't really remember, and that is how he came to be in the band with Steve and me."

"Where are you going to meet Jax for lunch today?"

I started laughing. "Oh, a place he detests." I continued laughing. "The Witch's Brew, do you know it?"

Iver laughed, too. "I do, the vegan restaurant with all the crystals in the window. Is Jax into all that stuff?"

I laughed even harder, finding it hard to breathe. "No," I finally gasped out. "He hates it."

Iver kept laughing too. "Well done, little minx. But I have a better idea."

I stopped laughing. "I'm listening."

"How about we zip to a local boutique and get you the finest looking outfit money can buy, and meet him on my territory, an expensive restaurant but not exclusive, and you can pull up in the Cobra? That will have his mouth dropping open in shock, I'll bet."

I sat up, excited. "Yes," I said excitedly, clapping my hands. "Usually, I do myself up in the look I use for the stage. You know it, Goth, black eyeliner. I need to up my game face. But you have to come with me, please, Iver. I don't think I could pull it off without you."

"I would be honored to escort you, Bella."

Chapter 9

Isabelle

Shopping with a man was a whole new experience. I saw myself in a way I never had before. Iver took me to a place a friend of his owned, a specialty boutique that also carried accessories and shoes. I walked out wholly redone and then some.

Iver purchased a cocktail dress for me, an evening gown, and of course, both came outfitted entirely with shoes and jewelry. The outfit I chose for lunch was a navy pencil skirt and matching pumps, a white cami, and a button-down angora sweater with three-quarter sleeves.

The owner, Nancy, did up only the three middle buttons on my sweater, as was the style, and added long inverted triangle earrings in gold. A sapphire necklace in gold trim completed the look. When I was ready, even I was impressed. Poor Jax would be wondering if aliens had abducted me and traded me out for a new and improved model.

Gone was my dark eyeliner and eyeshadow, and in its place, a much lighter line in mica, and the eye shadow was in grey and silver and jade. The lipstick was pale pink. I barely recognized myself.

When Iver saw me, his jaw dropped. "Wow, Bella, you are simply gorgeous; you should be a model."

I blushed. "Now, let's not get carried away. Can you imagine what the guys would think if they saw me in this getup? Take a picture, Iver. I want to send it to Marshall and Steve." He did, and a moment later, my phone pinged with the photos.

"Stand together," Nancy said, "let me take a few of the both of you." Subconsciously, I must have taken a play out of Iver's book. We were both dressed in similar colors, my primary, his accent colors, and vice versa.

When my phone pinged a moment later, I was stunned. We looked like some Barbie and Ken super couple. Iver looked down from over my shoulder. "Hot. Hot. Hot," he said, "and you look pretty good too." He laughed. I hit him on the arm and joined him in laughing at my expense.

I was super stoked about pulling up in a half a million-dollar car, wearing a matching outfit. It appeared that the Cobra and I were one. I saw Jax on the steps of Craft but pretended not to so I could channel my inner nonchalant, rich goddess. Watching Jax from the corner of my eye, it was hard not to break down in peals of laughter. His face mimicked a cartoon character whose jaw had dropped and hit the ground.

Inside the restaurant, I was happy to let Iver carry the conversation. When he offered to tour Jax around the commercial spaces of Manhattan's corridor, I was thrilled. I knew Jax wasn't planning at looking into commercial real estate; he's said that to me on the phone, and here to Iver, as an excuse. Why not just call it what it was? As Jax had chosen commercial real estate as his window dressing for disguising his true purpose in meeting me for lunch, I decided to let him reap the benefit of his bullshit. I was genuinely enjoying watching him squirm for a change.

Watching the two of them, I was struck by how much the past forty-eight hours had changed me. If I hadn't met Iver, I would be at the Witch's Brew in my shoddy denim, forcing my brother to eat a vegan something and put up with my attitude.

It was funny that it didn't bother me, the way Iver had impacted me in such a short period. I felt like I'd know him forever, yet I didn't know anything about him except he was loaded and had exceptional taste in everything.

His way of dealing with Jax had way more impact than any of the shenanigans I'd tried. I watched Iver; he was a master at directing people and conversation. I could learn a lot from him. Despite the advantage, I'd gained, by the outfit, my date, the restaurant, and Jax's sulky attitude. He was coming around. I think he also realized that Iver's friendship could be an advantageous friendship for him.

With lunch done, Iver escorted me to a waiting car to take me to the spa. I thought he was full of shit, but I was going to get pampered for the day while he ran around Manhattan with Jax. Poor Iver, I almost felt bad for him having to spend time with my arrogant brother.

Before we parted, Iver pulled me in for a kiss. "Your shopping bags will be waiting for you in your apartment, Bella, and I think I would like to see you in that red gown tonight. Would you wear it for me?"

Before I could answer, Jax interrupted, "If dinner is that fancy, I will bow out. I only have what I'm wearing."

Iver waved a hand in a dismissive gesture. "I have a cousin. Don't worry; I can hook you up. I'm sure Bella wouldn't want you to miss our evening." He smiled at his words, his gaze on me. The amusement was evident in his eyes.

"He's right, Jax," I added. "Please come. I have to go. You gents have fun, and I will see you at..."

"We'll pick you up at seven," Iver responded. "Your spa time is a few hours, with some downtime before then, in case you feel like napping. Isabelle, if there is anything specific you want, they are happy to accommodate. That also goes for drinks, snacks, merchandise, whatever you want, just ask."

"I will." I winked as I got in the car and left an amused Iver on the sidewalk with my brother, who was gazing at me with an unreadable stare. I spoke to my driver, sat back, and ran the lunch back over, replaying the funny parts over and over again until committed to memory.

I always wanted to remember this day; at least I would have that. If nothing else remarkable happened in the next few days with Iver and we parted ways, I would always have today and knowing that Iver, tonight, would probably outdo lunch. I rubbed my hands in anticipation of an evening of gloating.

Chapter 10

Iver

"Let's drive to the corridor, and we can park your car in one of the underground garages. We can start the tour from there."

I gave Jax the address and jumped in the Cobra, waited for him to get in his car, then we pulled out. It was a typical early afternoon in Manhattan, busy. But it was only 2:00; we would be parked by the time rush hour started.

I got busy with Bluetooth, reserving an additional spot for dinner and making reservations for Jax to get outfitted, transportation, a hotel room for Jax, the works, and by the time we pulled into the garage, the plans for the evening were in motion. Now all I had to do was tour the guy on his little investment charade and get to know him better.

He had been very reserved so far during our interactions, probably thinking that he was keeping me from getting to know anything significant about him. But he didn't know that I had immortal gifts that allowed me to see more of his character than he realized.

The shock he'd shown on the steps to the restaurant, had shifted immediately. He had been pondering me since we met, and I knew he wondered why Isabelle seemed altered and if the change was real or a put on for his benefit.

Jax was a smart guy; he was careful and had a good poker face. I also had a good poker face, and I could also cloak my intentions, which would have led to more confusion for poor Jax, as he couldn't get a read on me. I didn't really care. What I needed was information on the family, and I was hoping as head of the household, he could give it to me.

We parked; I stepped out of my car and waited for Jax to do the same. We engaged in small talk in the elevator, on the way up to the top floor of the building. I owned the entire building; he didn't know that. However, as my business took up only the top two levels, I had alluded that I had offices, not buildings.

Wait until he found out I owned the entire block. Well, not personally, my company held the neighborhood we were in and many others besides. I'd called Los Angeles home for the past forty years and kept my Malibu home for when I needed a surf and sun time out.

During that time, I created and purchased multiple companies on the eastern seaboard. Moving there to pursue Ariel was a natural choice.

I created enough subsidiaries in alternate names for the business that kept me from being easy to pinpoint as the head of the multi megalith corporation it was. I enjoyed my anonymity and intended to keep it. Besides, it was easier to control an empire that stretched into the millenniums if one held a low profile.

I was old money, original, blueblood money, and I looked like I'd grown my ancestors' fortunes; it was a good cover and far enough removed from any royal lineage that I was not a target for the royals.

When we arrived on the top floor of knightly acquisitions, I invited Jax into my office. The view was breathtaking. Jax lost his poker face for a moment as he took in the city skyline. While he stared out the window, I asked my personal assistant, Cheryl, to bring me in all of the lease spaces in the area.

Usually, she would have shared this information in a Google file that I could simply access from wherever, but I wanted to go old school and give Jax something concrete that he could hold in his hands.

Without taking his eyes away from the view, he asked, "What are you doing with my sister?" I hadn't expected to answer that question until later in the day. I guess Jax decided by asking me early in our conversation, he'd throw me off balance.

He'd decided to strike out. But I knew what he was doing; he was deflecting away from his discomfort in being sorely outclassed. I wanted him unstable and uncomfortable.

"I lost a bet," I answered with such a straight face that it incited him to spin around from the window's reflection and glare in shock directly into my eyes.

"You son of a bitch."

I held up my hands in mock surrender. "I was only saying what you were thinking, Jax. You don't give your sister much credit, do you?"

That stopped him. He slid into a seat opposite me. "No, but it's been years since Isabelle was a sweet kid. I don't know what happened, but one day, it was like a light switch flipped, and she's been a challenge ever since."

I wanted to slam him with the truth, but I thought I would wait for that. While he had his shield dropped, I decided to take another track. "Where are your parents? I was surprised to learn that Isabelle has no memory of her mother and only vague impressions of her father. Was there an accident, or was she adopted?"

A lot was hinging on his answer. I had looked up the family name, and it had no history. That meant they'd changed it at some point, but I couldn't find out anything, even with my connections. I should have found a trail, but there was nothing.

His eyes took me in, sizing me up. What did I look like to him? He was older than I, in the human world, but I was one of the oldest on the planet, and despite my youthful appearance, my eyes and demeanor spoke of a much older and wiser person.

"You are one of them, aren't you?"

I didn't know what I was expecting him to say, but that wasn't it. "I'm sorry, one of who?"

"Oh please, drop the charade. I knew when you got out of the car, you were not who you appeared to be. You're one of those guys who thinks it's fun to grab a fairly innocent girl and turn her into your plaything. You are dominant, looking for a poor, stupid girl to be your submissive, right?"

I couldn't help it. The laughter erupted from me. I mean, the relief of Jax not knowing I was an immortal being and assuming I was a predator was perfect. He had also shown me his hand; now, I knew what he thought of me.

"I don't find your laughing humorous in the least. If you're wondering about our parentage because you don't want to look bad in the society papers by hanging out with a girl who has a record or something, you won't find anything. Isabelle is clean."

I finally calmed down and, standing up, offered him a beverage, "Scotch?"

He nodded. I poured us each a tumbler and handed one to him. "Yes and no, in answer to your question. Yes, I am dominant, and no, I wasn't wondering if Isabelle's past would come to haunt me and somehow ruin my public reputation. If you search for me, you will find I do not have one. I remain hidden in the folds of business, as I have no interest in being in the tabloids or social media. I like my privacy, and I intend to keep it. As far as my proclivities go, Isabelle is submissive, and right now, we are enjoying each other's company. She is a strong woman, and I'm not interested in controlling her as a woman, or her career, unless she asks me to. I'm more interested in fulfilling a piece for her that has been missing."

"Oh yeah, and what's that?" Jax asked with a smirk.

"The ability to safely be herself."

He dropped the smirk. "What do you mean by *be herself?*"

In answer, I went in hard, as part of the discovery was pushing if I wanted answers, and I did. I would need to show him that I meant business.

"Who is Robert Voss?"

His reaction was entirely unexpected. "I don't know what you heard, but he was a guy I knew from school; we played on the football team together. Why?"

So, he was in denial, poor guy; this was going to hurt. "Are you still friends?"

"No. There was an altercation," Jax sighed, placing his empty glass down on my desk. "Robert was an amazing athlete with a huge ego. He was not a particularly nice guy, but he was always there for his brothers, fellow players. One day, I came home and found Finn, my younger brother, lying on the couch, all beat up. When I asked him what happened, he said that Robert had jumped him. I went after Robert and beat the crap out of him."

His gaze shifted from me to out the window, getting lost in the landscape once again. "The off thing of it," he continued, "Robert laughed the entire time and said it was a taste. A taste of what, I couldn't tell you as I wailed on him until he passed out, but he never told me anything more."

"So, you never found out why he beat up your brother?"

"No, I didn't. We moved a few months later, from Brooklyn to Jersey. Isabelle wanted a change going into high school, and as she seemed to be struggling, I thought, why not. I think we all wanted a change. As I'm sure you have learned, Jersey has a completely different vibe than Brooklyn."

I laughed. "That it does."

"Okay, I answered your question, now you answer mine."

"I'm not answering anything until I know more about your family. Why don't you exist beyond the three of you? Even your parents are names only, and there is no thread leading them to anywhere. It's almost as if you made up names to give to yourselves."

Jax sat back. Dropping his game face, he appeared older now, and tired. He'd been holding on to a secret, and the weight of it had stolen his youth. I briefly felt empathy for his plight and wondered if Issy was the only family member who may be immortal.

"I will be candid with you, Iver, but know I am putting Isabelle at risk by telling you anything."

He waited for me to respond, probably hoping with the mention of danger, I would back off, but I had no intention of doing that. I needed to know if his sister was my fated mate.

He sighed and continued. "What I'm about to tell you will sound crazy, but I have no idea who our family is. Before my father passed, he told me that it was important to stay hidden. That there were bad people in the world who didn't like us and would try to hurt us if they knew what we were. I, to this day, have no idea what he was talking about. I age and bleed like everyone else."

He stopped talking and regarded me. For my part, my game face was firmly in place; he wasn't getting any reaction out of me.

Sighing, he continued. "I don't know about Finn and me, but my father said Isabelle was special. Again, nothing has ever happened to show me she is anything but what she is. When she was seventeen and totally into drums as her career, I let her move to the city. Finn was here, too, at that time, so I thought she would be safe. And now you're here, so what do you want to know, Iver?"

"Have you heard the Catholic story of the fallen?"

His eyes rounded. "You mean God's fallen angels who came to Earth and became demons?"

I flinched. "Yes, that story, although demons is a bit much, don't you think? I always felt the story was created that way as a rulebook to control humans. After all, if there were a horrible negative force out there that could convince them to commit sins, then they would have to practice saintly virtues to remain clean. What a great way to control the actions of the human race. Historically speaking, the Catholic Church did an amazing job of instilling fear into people."

He laughed. "Yes, the church has done more for the patriarchal society that ruled here for hundreds of years than God could have, I think."

I eyed him. "You're buying what I'm saying; I didn't expect that."

He nodded, reaching into his pocket and pulling out a stone. At first glance, it appeared to be a stone, but on closer inspection, the material was like nothing I had ever seen. Understanding dawned in my eyes when I realized what he was holding.

"Is this a piece of the Leviathan ax?" I asked.

Jax smiled for the first time that day. "You know it."

"Of course, I know it; I was witness to its completion. The ax was imbued with incredible power by its maker; I can feel it from my seat, pulsating with a life of its own."

Jax was looking very confused.

"Listen, Jax, this relic is the physical embodiment of the two axes of thought within Christendom. The vertical ax of divinity and revelation, and the horizontal ax of loyalty and obedience. Legend says, when the two axes align, the secrets of the universe are unlocked. How did your family come by it, and why do you carry it around in your pocket. Are you mad?"

Jax's eyes were round as saucers. "How could you have seen the double-ended ax, Iver? I thought it was a myth or an idea, a story that put ideas into an object for teaching lessons and telling the story of creation."

While he'd been speaking, the piece of ax had been calling to me. I needed to touch it to feel its power. The part I had at home in my vault responded to my touch. His piece was the other half of mine; I was sure of it. I held out my hand, and Jax handed it to me.

I felt the strength of its vibration, the power brought me to my knees and then lifted me until both it and I were hovering in space, light pouring from it and filling me with its power, singing in my veins, surrounding me in ethereal light. As fast as it happened, it ended. I dropped back to Earth, in this case, the floor and casually handed the ax piece back to Jax, as if nothing odd had just occurred.

"Who the hell are you?"

"My name has no translation into English; I have gone with the Scandinavian, Iver, meaning bow warrior."

Jax sat back, his face drained of all color. "So, you are how old?"

"Millenniums, but my father is older."

"The question is, Jax, how old are you?"

"Huh? Oh, I'm a normal human, thirty-four years old."

"But your family were, are, guardians of a secret relic, why?

"I would love another glass of your scotch."

I chuckled. Fair enough, things were getting pretty intense, and the guy needed to cope. I refilled his tumbler and handed it back to him. He immediately chugged down half and sat back with a sigh, letting the seventy-eight-year-old scotch do its thing.

"That's better. I don't know much. My parents died unexpectedly, and I often wonder if their death wasn't an accident. Any knowledge died with them. All I know is this relic has to remain secret until the savior arrives; the savior will restore all that was lost, or something like that, whatever that means. I don't know, Iver, I was young and had two younger siblings to raise. I have this ax thing and what I told you; that is all I know."

I searched him for lies and came up with none; he felt he was sharing all he knew. But his subconscious knew more than his conscious mind was allowing. That meant that at some point, he had made a promise not to reveal the stone's importance. A promise made to a fallen was binding. For me to learn everything Jax knew, I would have to unravel the thread that led back to that person. Or break the thread entirely. I couldn't do that, but my father could.

"Jax, I want you to say that you promise not to share who and what I am with anyone. Is that clear?"

"Yes, I promise not to reveal your secret."

I was feeling confident with the thread I'd just created with Jax. I relaxed back in my seat.

"So, how about that real estate?" He laughed. "I'm sure you know that was my excuse for meeting with Isabelle. I have no such venture in mind, but this is stunning. I would love to branch out. But this is way beyond anything I could ever afford."

"Maybe not," I answered cryptically. "I have a feeling that you and I will become family one day, and family helps each other. I would love to have you closer to your sister, and you should be aware of why you two have become estranged."

He nodded his head for me to continue.

"Robert Voss needs to be found and eliminated. He raped your sister, and I want him in jail for the rest of his life or dead. I'd prefer death."

Jax, who had just taken a sip of his whiskey, coughed it

back up, spewing it in a trajectory around him. "What are you saying? Issy doesn't even know Robert, other than the few times he came around the house, and she must have been ten or eleven at the time."

"Wait, are you saying that Robert raped Issy when she was a child?"

His wan expression went from shock to fury in under three seconds. "I will fucking kill him!"

Jax jumped out of his chair and stomped around the room, looking like an enraged bull. I could see why Isabelle would have had a problem with this growing up. Jax would be intimidating to a female when he was controlled by rage. I wondered if that was why he was single.

I got up and poured more whiskey. I placed it back on the table instead of handing Jax his glass directly. I didn't need a glass chucked through my window. I waited about another thirty seconds, and then, using my ability to modulate and control, I said, "Sit down, Jax. Drink your whiskey and calm yourself."

He did as I commanded, but not robotically, as one may expect from a command that someone didn't want to obey. My tone delved into his subconscious and acted as a soothing psychological and emotional massage. He sat down, drank the whiskey, and blew out a breath, instantly calming down. Closing his eyes briefly, he mumbled, "Great trick."

"When faced with a rampaging bull, it comes in handy. Now tell me all you know about this piece of shit, because when we find Robert, we'll kill him together."

Chapter 11

Jax

"**A**re you saying what I think you're saying?" Jax asked with disbelief in his voice. "I'm not sure what shocks me more, the fact you have learned more about my sister in a few days than I have in the past nine years, or that you are up for murder."

Iver gave me an even look. "This is righting a wrong. If this turns out to be a case of misdeed while the rest of his life has been rosy, then so be it, we will find a just punishment. But, I suspect, he is a person without conscience."

I suddenly felt very weary and old. Thinking of my age reminded me that I was sitting beside an immortal, who had lived several millennia and didn't look a day over thirty. "I guess when you're immortal, stress doesn't affect your age, because you look pretty good for an old guy."

Iver was watching me with his blue ice eyes, his expression blank. "If you could be an immortal, would you?"

I laughed. "If only, I could live a good thousand years and still not accomplish all I would like to do in this short life. But I guess in retrospect, if we didn't agonize over how short life is, we wouldn't appreciate it as much. What are your thoughts on living beyond the normal scope of time, Iver?"

He leaned back in his chair, reminding me of a scene from a movie I'd once seen, the Godfather. Of course, nothing about the man resembled Al Pacino or Robert DeNiro, but his attitude did. He reminded me of a king, or maybe a kingpin, with his mafia swagger. It boiled down to the empire. The man could and did run an empire, and it exuded from him.

"There may be a way this could happen." He ignored my question, going back to his on my mortality. I was lost in thought and almost missed his words. "I'm sorry, there is a way for what precisely?"

"You know, to become immortal."

The words hung between us like ripe fruit that I was afraid to pick from the branch. Dare, I hope? I closed my eyes, no longer trusting that sense to help me navigate these uncharted waters.

"Okay, Iver, I'll bite, how do I become immortal?" I asked, keeping my eyes closed. If this was a joke and he was kidding, I didn't want to see it. Hearing it would be bad enough, as if I could be immortal. I'm pretty sure that it was an exclusive club to which you couldn't gain an invitation just because you wanted it.

"Well, I may have said that incorrectly. I meant that you may be an immortal, like Isabelle and me."

My eyes flew open, looking for confirmation that Issy was also immortal. "What?" I croaked as a sip of scotch had gone down the wrong way and I was gasping.

Iver laughed; he was like a geyser erupting. I couldn't help but join in once I'd recovered, then he explained. "Until this meeting, I only suspected who Isabelle was. You have provided the missing piece to confirm my suspicions that Isabelle is the immortal I'm to find and protect."

"How so?"

This day was becoming too much. I held out my glass, laughing. "As if, really, Iver, how could Issy possibly have so much value? She is a selfish, indulgent rock star wannabe. She plays at night and sleeps all day and does whatever she wants."

Iver leaned forward, his energy suddenly becoming aggressive. "Listen up, Isabelle is the descendant of a pure angel. Ariella, the first female king of the Sumerians, and Apollo, the Roman god. Ariella must have placed Ariel—Isabelle—in with one of her unknown descendants. I'm not sure if that is your mother or your father or possibly both. They would not have entrusted anyone with the secrets they have given you, Jax, even if you don't remember them. They would not entrust just a human with the Leviathan ax and the life of a first-generation fallen."

He paused for a moment and then went on. "You, Jax, had better get used to the fact that your sister is the hope for immortals on this planet. If she dies before her time, then all the immortals will die with her. She has to stay alive and create the next line of immortals with me. If you want to see a future beyond mortality, then you'd better wise up sooner rather than later and make up with your sister. She hasn't done anything wrong anyway; you did."

It was my turn to get my back up and send a little aggressive energy his way. "How do you figure?"

"Easy, you never took care of her, and you never protected her. The most valuable life on the planet was left to fend for herself. And, if you had been kinder to her, she would have been more inclined to stay. You lost her when you stopped loving her and spending time with her. What happened with Robert happened after you turned your back on her, Jax."

He was right. I sat back in my chair again, sliding my hand over my eyes. I couldn't deny his words. I knew I had let Issy down; I'd listened to my excuses and taken the easy path. I preferred to avoid her than to help her.

"Okay, let's say I accept what you're saying. How do you expect me to repair anything with Issy? She hates me."

"You're a grown man, Jax; I'm sure you can figure it out. But I will give you one tip. Stop calling her Issy; she hates it. She associates it with her past and with Robert and Brooklyn. She used to look up to you. At some point, you stopped being her hero. I don't know what nosedive your life took, and I don't want to. Just begin mending your relationship with your sister. Tonight, is a good time to start. Speaking of," Iver glanced at his watch, "it's time for your fitting."

Chapter 12

Isabelle

I was lying on my front, having a massage, and thinking about my life. In a few short days, Iver had turned me into a spoiled princess. I could certainly get used to this. *You will,* a voice uttered. My inner goddess had gotten on board with Iver. She was prancing in a gown, wearing a diamond tiara and beckoning me to try a life I'd never dreamed or thought I wanted for myself.

I moaned as Lillith worked the knots out of my back and shoulders.

She giggled. "I'm glad you are enjoying this. Iver asked specifically for me."

Wait; what? She must have felt me tense.

"Sorry, I meant to say he specifically asked for my services for you. He said you are a drummer and needed a bit more than the typical relaxing Swedish massage that you would normally get at our spa."

"Okay, thanks for clarifying," I managed to get out with yet another moan. "I haven't known Iver long, and I have to admit, I was curious about his usual type. You know, what type of woman does he send here?"

I was digging, hoping that Lillith had worked on other women that Iver had sent to the spa.

"I can't help you with that. I either have never met anyone Iver sent here, or maybe you are the first; for me, at least I know you are the first."

She meant her words to be encouraging, but all they did was raise more questions. Did Iver have a type? Had he sent other women here? I still didn't know why he'd chosen me. I was a pretty average person, average in looks, height, nothing special.

But the way he looked at me made me feel like a cross between a movie star and a seductress. Iver made me feel like I was a queen. I wonder if he did that for all of his other women? Ugh, the thought of him with other women pissed me off, and I was here to relax. I tried to put the Iver parade of women out of my mind.

"Lillith, do you know what I'm having done next?"

She paused. "Let me look at your itinerary. Steam capsule, manicure, pedicure, hair, and makeup, wow, the full meal deal. You must be going out on a date tonight?" She looked up from the list on the tablet.

I lifted my head and grinned. "Yes, and I'm supposed to be wearing a gown, so I guess it is something special."

"I wonder if you are going to the Renaissance Ball," Lillith asked excitedly.

I rolled onto my side and asked, "What on earth is a Renaissance Ball?"

"It's like a Governor's Ball; people fly in from all around the world to attend, and it's by invitation only. They call it an invitation, but at fifteen hundred dollars per plate, I'd say it's a private fundraiser for political parties. Usually, presidential elections have dinners like that, where political big-wigs who can sway votes gather to schmooze with the governor or president-elect."

"You seem well informed," I said, sitting up.

Lillith blushed. "My grandfather will be at the Renaissance Ball tonight."

"Lillith, can you bring up the Renaissance Ball on the tablet?"

"Sure, just give me a sec."

She found the website and brought the tablet over to me. We oohed and awed over photos from previous events. I scrolled down until I found the organizers. There was only one, Fallen Enterprises.

I tried looking up Fallen Enterprises, to see who the CEO or president of the company was, but I couldn't find anything about them. It was as if a ghost owned the company. I smelled a mystery; could Iver be part of Fallen Enterprises?

Continuing to look, I found one obscure article on like page four of my Google search. I knew it was a tech company, and I knew that Iver was a tech mogul. Could this be his gala we would be attending?

Beside me, Lillith seemed suddenly edgy. "I'd better get you to the steam showers, Isabelle, or we will be behind schedule."

"Sure." I offered the tablet back and couldn't help giving her a penetrating glance. "Are you sure you have never met Iver?" I asked point-blank.

She blanched and then blushed. "No." she answered, but she wouldn't make eye contact with me, so I gathered that she was full of it. She quickly left, and someone else came back to usher me down to the steam and give me instructions, hanging a fluffy robe and bath sheet on the hanger for when I finished up in the shower. Then she left, and I was alone, feeling unsettled and wondering who Iver was.

I quickly forgot my anxiety when I went for my mani/pedi, as I engaged in witty banter with my technician. She was a petite little Filipino lady with the biggest personality. I knew, to work for a high caliber spa paid well, but I still left her a tip, mostly because I appreciated her lightening the mood and spoiling me with Bailey coffees and Godiva chocolates.

My next stop was with a James Dean look-alike who channeled his inner diva. He was as queer as they came, he said, and I simply adored him. What would have come off as insulting with someone else, made me laugh when he made fun of my short, Goth locks.

Maybe that was the idea behind the Bailey's and chocolates, to soften me up for Jimmy. Because I had short hair already, I didn't think there was much he could do to change my look. Imagine my shock when what he did to it really *did* change the look. He gave me streaks and styled it back in a fancy coif, instead of my hair spilling forward, covering my eyes.

When I was allowed to look in the mirror at the finished product, I looked older, mature, and pretty sexy. I liked it. During the makeover, someone brought champagne and appetizers. So, by the time I left the spa, I was feeling carefree, not drunk, but relaxed.

I was escorted to the car by Iver's driver whom he had called for me. But before I stepped inside the car, I felt the hairs on the back of my neck rise. Someone was watching me. I looked around, checking doorways and windows, but saw no one.

Like the previous night, I knew someone was there. I briefly thought of Robert Voss, the perfect stalker. He would suddenly appear out of doorways and scare the shit out of me when I was a child. Whoever was watching me, I prayed it wasn't him.

I watched for another moment, but still, I saw no one lurking. I sighed and allowed Benson to help me into the car. He must have sensed my agitation and kept up a steady chatter on the way to my apartment.

Benson escorted me to the front door, before taking his leave, and he didn't pull away into traffic until I was safely inside. When I unlocked my apartment door, I found all the items from our shopping trip lying over on the couch.

I wondered how Iver had managed to get my items inside the apartment. He must have rung the manager, I surmised. I grabbed a bottle of water from the fridge and discovered that my fridge was full of groceries. I laughed. Did the guy have a magic wand?

The kitchen counter was clean, and I was pretty sure it had been dirty when I left yesterday. Then I glanced around and discovered my entire bachelor pad, the whole place, was clean. How had I missed that?

Well, hell, I wasn't going to complain. I hated cleaning. I looked at the time. I had an hour until Iver and Jax would pick me up.

I texted Iver.

Me: *How did you get in my apartment?* frowning emoji

Iver: *How do you think?* winky face emoji

Me: *You promised sexual favors to old Frank, the apartment manager?* laughy emoji

Iver: *I love it when you tease.* heart emoji

Me: *So, this is the right time to say having my apartment cleaned is too much, and I will not be joining you this evening.* pouty face emoji

I waited; five minutes went by, and I was beginning to think that maybe what I 'd said was pushing it.

Iver: *I see someone wants a* spanking emoji *and* devil emoji

Me: laughing face emoji

Iver: *Don't forget, Isabelle, no underwear, or that play spanking will not feel too playful.*

Me: sticking out tongue emoji

. . .

I put my phone down and headed to my closet, hanging up the garment bags that had been laid down so carefully on the couch, with nothing to do but get dressed. I removed the gown from the protective bag and put it on.

I looked so sophisticated, and it was such a different look for me. A voice echoed, *there you are, no more hiding.* I glanced around the room, expecting to see a specter. Then I laughed; my imagination was working overtime.

The plunging neckline did wonders for my chest, one of my best features. I slid on the shoes next and practiced walking. I didn't usually wear a thin heel when I wore heeled shoes. I usually went with the chunky ones and wedges so I had better balance, but that look wouldn't do with this elegant dress.

Next, I put on the necklace that Iver had given me to go with the gown. It wasn't in the store, and he'd produced it before we had left to go shopping. I think he picked the dress to go with the necklace.

The chain was a series of precious jewels and stones, and in the very center was a small shape that looked almost like the Egyptian ankh but in the form of a woman's body. It was unique, and with the gown, I looked like a princess. Was that Iver's intention, to make me look like a princess?

He could make me look like one, but he couldn't make me act like one. I was who I was, and this was not me. Despite looking more fabulous than ever before, I didn't appreciate feeling like a visitor.

I would have to let him know that if he was looking to get me to fall in love with him, this was not the way to do it. Except I would have to wait until later, as Jax would be with us, and the last thing I wanted was to be tag-teamed by those two.

I mean, after their bro afternoon, I'm sure they were tight, and I would be the third wheel on this little outing. Despite the game, we were playing at Jax's expense. I did feel some warmth in my heart, seeing the two of them together. Who knows, maybe if Iver and I worked out, those two could become friends. I tried to picture Sunday dinners together as a family and ended up laughing so hard at the image.

I turned away from the mirror. My wonderful afternoon, and suddenly turning, I was sad, and I didn't know why. My day was like the Cinderella, billionaire romance stories I read. The too good to be true stories that were pure fantasy, which, of course, is why I enjoyed them so much, I mean, why not fantasize a bit? In every story, there is an obstacle to overcome. What would impede my love story?

The answer to my question was like an explosion in my head. *You, you are the problem, Isabelle.* Yeah, I was, and that was okay. If Iver wanted me, even with all my issues, then so be it. I would be a full participant in the next few days. But what were the chances of anything monumental occurring tonight to shake me out of my funk?

I finished my bottle of water and placed it in my recycle bin. I grabbed my phone to text Iver when it pinged.

Iver: *We are downstairs, my lady, and your chariot awaits.*
  Me: *On my way.*

I took one last look in the mirror and blew out a breath. I had butterflies in my stomach. I didn't know why, but I felt like tonight was a test of some sort, and deep down, I wanted to pass it. I wanted to be swept off my feet repeatedly and have the happy ending that I read about in my books.

I grabbed my phone and my evening bag, locked my door, and headed down the stairs. Both Jax and Iver were standing on the sidewalk, waiting to escort me. Jax looked fantastic, very handsome. I bet the single ladies would be checking him out wherever we were going. And Iver looked like a god, gorgeous. Too gorgeous, I would have to keep my eye on him.

When they saw me, a big grin spread across Iver's face, and I received a whistle of appreciation from my brother.

"Isabelle, you are stunning," Jax said, leaning in and kissing my cheek."

"Thank you, and you look fantastic. Maybe after tonight, you won't be single anymore." He laughed. "I'm not looking to change my status anytime soon."

Iver lifted my hand and kissed the back of it and then turned it over and kissed my palm. It was very intimate, and when he did it, the connection felt like a zing to my core. He lifted his head, grinning like an errant schoolboy who had gotten away with a nasty trick.

"Isabelle, you look like a goddess. I am the luckiest man on the planet."

I blushed. "You remember that, when I have to beat all the women off you with a stick, Iver. You are too good looking for your own good."

He laughed at my comment but pulled me in for a gentle hug, mindful of not creasing my gown. "No stick required; I can be very standoffish."

"Really? Another one of your many tricks?"

He helped me into the limousine. "No Benson tonight?" I asked.

"He is my daily driver; I have someone else for nights."

"Seriously? Iver, you and I need to have a conversation about your assets; you may be too rich for me." I was joking, but I wanted to see what his reaction would be.

"Certainly, I can arrange to have the most recent reports done up in a spreadsheet for you. But only if you agree to marry me. I can't have any trade secrets leaking out."

It was his turn to joke and watch for my reaction. My heart skipped a beat when he said the word *marry.* "I'm sure," I replied, glossing over his proposal. "What does marriage look like to you, barefoot, pregnant every two years, and waiting for my loving husband to come home from work?"

Jax, on my other side, was smirking but not participating in our little marriage verbal sparring.

Iver seemed to consider my words. "Mmm, I'm in no rush to procreate, and when I am, one or two is plenty. Maybe in ten or fifteen years; I want you all to myself first. And, I imagine that your band will become a huge success and you won't want to have children before you're ready to slow down a little. I imagine you touring all over the world and me having to follow you around when time allows."

I was shocked that he'd given some thought to us together and imagined me in his life as a musician. He didn't plan on changing me at all; he was going to change in an attempt to maintain the humorous bantering.

I responded, "You can't do that, Iver, you are a tech mogul, and I'm sure your company needs you. There will be no time to chase around a little nobody like me."

He changed in an instant, going from humorous to angry. His only outward expression was his eyes. They became intense and glittered as he stared into my eyes. "I think I was obvious with you, regarding those self-deprecating comments. You are far from being a little nobody, and if I catch you making that remark again, you won't be sitting down comfortably for days."

I was shocked at the intensity in his tone. I expected Jax to have a comment. But he said nothing, using his silence as a way to deflect. I commented in his direction. "Nothing to say, brother? Aren't you going to at least pretend to care and tell my big bossy boyfriend he can't do that, or you'll beat him up?"

He gazed down at me. "Isabelle, I love and will always love you. But this is between you and Iver, and I know you hold all the power here. You don't need me to save you."

I was speechless. Had that come out of my ornery brother's

mouth? Iver must have talked with him during their afternoon together. He never called me by my full name, and he hadn't said 'I love you' in forever.

I was thrown off balance by both of them. "That's right; I have the power, and don't you two forget it."

Feeling as if I'd won, I was happy to sit back and enjoy the rest of the ride. "Uh, except I have no idea where we are going. Where is the restaurant?"

Chapter 13

Iver

I t was hard to keep a straight face when she asked which restaurant we were going to, but I dared not laugh. After all, Isabelle did hold power. She set the rules for our little game, and she could pull the plug at any time.

"We aren't going to a restaurant; we are attending a ball."

Both Jax and Isabelle cranked their heads to look at me. Jax's eyes held many questions; he was easy to read. Her eyes held amusement; somehow, she'd figured it out.

"Let me guess, the Renaissance Ball?"

I made a mental note to talk to my staff at the Sumer Spa, where I'd sent Isabelle for her afternoon pampering session. Someone had mentioned the ball to her, and I wanted to know who.

"Yes, we are going to the Renaissance Ball. Of course, *Renaissance Ball* is a misleading name. One would think we are dressing in period clothing. The title refers to the idea of the renaissance man, and of course, woman. The idea that those most clever and dedicated to the concept and understanding

that higher thought is paramount to living and our environment. Also, gifted individuals who have gained attention
through their works versus through their money, although
money is not a barricade to attendance. Quite the opposite, at
fifteen hundred dollars per plate, you have to have some excess
coin floating around, to attend the event."

My explanation ignited more questions with Jax, not less as
I'd hoped.

Turning to face me, he asked, "Why would you want to
take Isabelle and me to such an event? Don't these things
usually have politicians at them who are looking for campaign
money?"

I laughed. "Yes, and no, Jax. Traditionally, political balls
would attract those individuals interested in running or who
have already thrown their hat into the race. But in this case,
this is sponsored by businesses. Many start-ups attend because
it allows them to meet some of the enterprising moguls and not
just in this city, either. People attending this event are seeking
opportunities—artists, musicians, tech, gaming, and, yes, business. To summarize, companies and individuals seeking knowledge and opportunity to partner in a more profound hub."

"And let's not forget the most important piece of the
puzzle," Isabelle commented.

"What's that?" Jax responded.

She smiled smugly. "The company that is putting on the
event, and has for these past ten years, is Iver. Isn't that right?"

The little minx, she had used her time to learn about an
event that she didn't even know she was attending. Her
instincts were sharp, and I was learning that Isabelle, despite
her outward Gothic appearance, was harboring a renaissance
woman.

"Now you see, Jax," I said to him but looking at Isabelle,
"your sister is a perfect example of a renaissance woman. She
has researched an event that she's heard about but didn't know

she was attending and looked deep enough to know that it was being put on by one company. My question is, Isabelle, what makes you think it is my company?"

She laughed. "That's the easy part. You said you don't like attention, and you like to remain anonymous. So, when I realized that I couldn't access any information regarding the owners of Fallen Enterprises, I knew it must be you."

I chuckled with her. "You will be my undoing, Ms. Isabelle."

Jax redirected the conversation, and for the rest of the car ride, the siblings poked fun at what Isabelle perceived was going to be a room full of dressed up fraternity houses from the best universities in the country.

I did little to deter them in their mutual digging and enjoyed their easy banter. It was enjoyable, listening to the siblings, and for a brief moment, I was distracted from the burden of my existence.

I knew there would be descendants of Ariella's offspring in attendance, none, of course, like Isabelle, but I was curious to see if they would gravitate to each other.

Isabelle looked exactly like Ariella, except their coloring. Ariella was dark and had fit into the Middle Eastern culture well. One of her descendants, a woman I'd met around a hundred years ago, Fawzi, had the same green eyes as Isabelle.

Of course, Fawzi was dead now, but her granddaughter, Devi, would be in attendance tonight. She and Isabelle would be close to the same age. She worked for my company and spearheaded the charitable organizations branch.

Devi's superpower was trust. People, myself included, instinctually trusted Devi. She was good to have in the company, running projects that required large donations. I was looking forward to introducing her to Isabelle and her brother.

I was deep in thought when we pulled up to the mansion on the upper east side, the location of this year's ball. I had attended an art exhibit at the estate some years ago and fallen in love with it. Its vast gardens and the driveway provided a natural barrier between the historic property and the rest of the world.

My driver opened my door first and then walked around to Jax's side and opened his door. I helped Isabelle out from my side. She smoothed her gown with her hands, flashed me a million-dollar smile, and set off down the red carpet.

Jax leaned in. "I don't know what you've done with my sister. She is so changed, I hardly recognize her."

I smirked, "That is because, for her, this is all a game. She has given me only a few days to wow her off her feet. She is playing a role, not herself, or to be more specific, she is experimenting with another version of herself."

He laughed. "Let's hope it lasts. I like this version a lot better than the dark, pissed off one." He followed his sister down the red carpet. I watched the siblings, noticing that they shared a similarity in how they moved. Both graceful, but where Jax walked with purpose, Isabelle was more feline. She took her time, allowing people to stare and wonder who she was.

I grinned. I had my work cut out for me; that woman would keep me on my toes.

Chapter 14

Isabelle

When we stepped through the doors, my self-confidence flew out the window. Despite Iver's explanation on the type of people I should expect to see, he didn't really give me an idea of the calibre of the so-called artists.

Beside me, Jax whistled softly under his breath. We both had fallen through the rabbit hole. But unlike myself, Jax looked excited to be among the elite. This was probably a dream come true for him.

There must have been fifty people in the foyer, and all looking our way to check out the new arrivals. Jax put on his business smile while I stood beside him. Thankfully, Iver came up and flanked my other side.

I wondered what we three looked like to the fifty people in the lobby. There was one very young woman, on the arms of two very handsome men, one godlike in his appearance. Before I could ask Iver what the protocol was for the evening, we were introduced, "Jax Ackles, Iver Eriskay and date, Isabelle Ackles."

Curiosity settled, everyone turned back to their discussions.

"And date? Really, Iver?"

He chuckled. "Sorry, I wanted everyone to know you are taken."

Rolling my eyes, I replied, "In that case, why not just call me Isabelle Eriskay?"

"I thought about it," he mused, "but then thought how could we have a wedding and invite some of these folks if they thought we were already married?"

My eyes narrowed, but before I could give him a piece of my mind, Jax said, "I would love to stay and hear you two fight, but I have bigger fish to fry. Later, kids."

My brother moved toward the largest gathering, and the crowd swallowed him from sight. I had a very odd feeling that everyone in the room knew who I was. It was silly, as I was a nobody, why would anyone know me?

"Come, Princess Isabelle, let me escort you around the room. I know there are people here you are going to want to meet."

Hooking my arm through his, I allowed Iver to lead me around the lobby of the mansion. I met a senator, three mayors, and two artists, one of whom had his work in the Metropolitan Museum and on display in the lobby. He was a modern artist and, from what I could tell, was very good.

But I was no expert, and modern was not my cup of tea. I enjoyed portraits, landscapes, the last period in art history that I enjoyed was the impressionists. As far as art went, I was very old fashioned, considering my music tastes were purely eclectic and leaned as far in either way as possible.

I was intimidated by everyone I spoke with. Thankfully, trays of spirits were continually circulating, and I made sure that I got my fill. It took a lot to get me drunk. The wine I was drinking wouldn't cause me to get drunk nor mixing white, red, and champagne, which I'd already done. Iver gave me a look but said nothing.

What it did do is give me a little bit of bravery, enough to be playful with Iver. "Oh, darling," I gushed, "look, isn't that the new rap artist on Billboard's top fifty?"

He nodded. "Yes, Jacob Rea, his music is playing in all the New York clubs."

"Do be a good boy and introduce us."

"A good boy?" His eyebrow lifted. "What is going on with you?"

I giggled. "Going on? Why, nothing, but if you want me to play a role, which I am, then I'm going to play it how I want."

He grabbed my arm and gently marched me toward the kitchen and out the back, into the garden. He sat me down on a bench and squatted down in front of me. "Isabelle, what is wrong? Why do you need to play a role, why not just be yourself?"

I stood and kicked off my shoes, scrunching my toes in the fresh grass. I sighed in relief. "Because, Iver, I'm not a gown girl, a champagne girl, and walking around meeting five hundred strangers is not my idea of fun."

He reached out, grabbing my hand and pulling me onto his lap and sitting, in one smooth motion. "Isabelle, it's not what you think. I don't expect you to be a certain way. I was hoping you'd give everyone here a big dose of sassy Isabelle. I adore her, and I think everyone else would too."

I rolled my eyes. Iver chose to ignore my bratty eye roll and continued. "In about fifteen minutes, we are going to get the call to dinner. You are sitting beside Alan Partridge, and he is expecting to talk shop with you. If you still feel like a fish out of water when dinner is over, we will leave. Until then, can you please be yourself, bratty, pig-headed, stubborn, beautiful you?"

I laughed. "You know just what to say, don't you?"

He smiled indulgently at me.

"Fine, I will tone it down. I just don't like feeling like I'm on display."

"I understand, but I think that is you more than the crowd. I have been watching the way people react to you, and I can safely say no one is sizing you up. Quite the opposite, people seem quite happy to make your acquaintance. Let's go back in; I have someone I want you to meet, and no doubt she is wondering where we are."

"Great," I sighed, putting my heels back on. "Is this when I find out you're secretly married, or maybe hiding a harem of young, drugged up girls?"

He grinned at that. "I'm glad to see your sense of humor is working."

We entered through a side door, into a round room decorated as a library from the 1900s.

"Oh," I mumbled, coming to a halt. "This room is incredible, Iver, can't we just stay here?"

"Don't worry, Bella; we will come back and spend more time in this room after dinner. The collection is quite nice, but I think you will like my home library even more."

I let him pull me from the room, promising myself I would be back as soon as I could ditch him. We'd only taken a few steps down the hall when we spotted a young woman about my age, making her way down the hall in our direction.

"Iver, it's about time. I've been looking everywhere for you."

My hackles instantly rose. Whoever she was, her familiarity with Iver was annoying. The way she linked her arm in his and gave him a peck on the cheek. It didn't help that she was a petite, probably size zero, five-foot brunette seductress with exotic green, so dark as to be almost black, eyes.

"Devi, let me introduce you to the lovely Isabelle."

"Isabelle, it is nice to meet you," she said, extending her other hand, her left still firmly planted through Iver's. As she reached for my hand, her exotic green eyes, similar to my own, traveled to my necklace that Iver had given me. Her hand stopped moving and hovered between mine and looking as if she wanted to touch the ankh.

Looking into my eyes, she said, "May I?" I nodded, but as she touched it, I felt a power, and the necklace heated up and zinged her. I don't know how else to describe it. She quickly withdrew her hand. I had an immediate dislike, and apparently, so did my necklace. There was something about her I didn't trust, other than her arm wrapped around my boyfriend's.

Whoa, boyfriend, there I was having thoughts on Iver as being mine. *He is*, a voice spoke quietly, *he is all yours for the taking. Claim the demigod.* I was hallucinating, too many mixed beverages, I chided myself.

"Nice to meet you too; are you a friend or co-worker?"

"I've only been part of Fallen Enterprises for a year, but I also did my internship here. Iver is a friend of my parents. That is how we know each other."

Despite her words, her actions seemed contrary. "You'll have to excuse me for saying, but you seem unnaturally familiar with your boss. Do you always hang on to his arm at social events?" I don't know where that came from, and it hung in the air between her and me. I glanced up at Iver, who was watching the exchange with interest.

She quickly pulled her arm out from his. "I guess, well, yes, I suppose I do."

"You may want to rethink that," I said, looping my arm through his. "I wouldn't want people to mistake you for his girlfriend, as that role has been filled. It was very nice to meet you, Devi, I'm sure we'll see each other again."

With that, I steered Iver and myself down the hall, leaving her to watch our retreating backs.

Chapter 15

Isabelle

Iver escorted me to the dining room, one of three set up to accommodate all of the guests in attendance. As promised, I was seated beside Alan Partridge. His career began in a piano bar on the east side. There, he made friends with his now band and was discovered by New World Records.

He was the most sought out recording artist in the United States and had partnered with many big names. Those he didn't record with, he wrote for, and now he was on some music show on Fox. Alan stood. "Iver, it's good to see you," he said, reaching out his hand and shaking Iver's. "This must be Isabelle."

My hands were sweating; I was standing in front of one of the biggest stars in music history. I tentatively reached out my hand and shook Alan's in return. He had gentle energy, and his eyes were very inviting, looking into mine. I instantly relaxed. Nice trick that he seemed to have in common with Iver.

"Please sit, Isabelle, and tell me all about yourself." After pushing in my chair, Iver took the seat on the other side of me and struck up a conversation with an artist and his date, a gorgeous male model I was sure I'd seen in magazines.

During the next five courses, Alan and I talked about everything to do with music, history, role models, and influences. We hit it off; he had a relaxed, unrushed vibe about him that resonated with me.

He was the opposite of pretentious, confident in who he was, but not arrogantly so. Alan knew music, and he recognized talent. Before we parted, I made arrangements for the guys and me to stop by his recording studio for a tour and some studio time.

I warned him we had never recorded anything, that we'd only ever done live performances. He said he'd know in the first thirty seconds if we were worth his time. I was good with that; thirty seconds was better than an unknown future of trying to get ahead and hoping to be discovered.

I excused myself after the meal and headed toward the ladies' room. I sat down on a chaise lounge and texted Steve.

Me: *You will never guess who I met tonight.*

Steve: *Who?*

Me: *Alan friggin' Partridge, we just finished dinner. He's super cool.*

Steve: *What? Holy hell, that is amazing.*

Me: *Yeah, and we're invited to his studio for a tour and to do a bit of playing. If he likes us, he is going to work with us.*

Steve: *What? I gotta text Marshall. He is going to lose his shit!*

Me: laughy emoji *and* heart eyes emoji

Me: *Gotta go, will text you the details tomorrow, but tell Marshall to book off Monday all day.*

Steve: thumbs up emoji

. . .

I deposited my phone into my handbag and went and did my bathroom business. I was alone in the bathroom and liked the privacy; I was still processing dinner and the opportunity that had fallen in my lap. I laughed—fallen, as if. That was all Iver's doing. When I exited the bathroom, I walked the opposite direction from the party and toward the beautiful little library.

I poked my head in and was happy to see there was no one else there. I wandered around the space, touching books, and picking up the odd one. Mostly, I just immersed myself in the vibe of the room.

I loved how it felt, and if I ever got rich and built my own place, I would make a circular room like this to house my library. I was reading an inscription when I felt a prickling on the back of my arms.

Someone was watching me. Straightening up, I pretended that everything was excellent and casually glanced around the room to the doorway, but there was nobody there. My eyes traveled to the windows. I didn't see anyone at first; then, my eyes caught a glimpse of red. That was the color of the jackets that the parking attendants were wearing.

I turned my body and watched the window through my peripheral vision. Again, I saw red and followed it up to the face, to try to get a glimpse at my stalker. What I saw was straight from my nightmares; it was my childhood stalker, the face that had haunted me for almost ten years, Robert Voss.

Chapter 16

Iver

Being a direct descendant of a Fallen has given me immortality. Being the son of a goddess has imbued me with unique gifts that often come in handy. I could sense danger and intent. I could use my super-hearing to tap into multiple conversations at once. My father once said, 'Can you imagine what it must be like to be the all-powerful being who can hear all of humanity at once?'

Learning to stream conversations and detect essential words was a lot like the artificial intelligence the government was starting to develop and use. China had been doing this far longer than any other country, but every country was now developing this software, something I was born with naturally.

Isabelle had excused herself half an hour ago for the bathroom, and I was starting to worry. I scanned the mansion, listening for her voice. I couldn't pick it up in any room. Excusing myself from an intense art debate between the lovers beside me, I made my way toward the bathroom that Isabelle would have used, closest to our dining area.

I waited until it was empty and then entered; she had been here. A residue of her energy still lingered in the bathroom. I stood still; my ears were picking up nothing, but my senses were picking up panic. Isabelle was in trouble.

I ran down the hallway toward that circular library she had been eyeing earlier. I heard a scream. I ran through the door just in time to catch Isabelle from crashing to the floor. A flash of red caught my outer vision then disappeared.

I texted Jax.

Me: *Your sister has fainted. I am taking her to my place.*

Jax: *Do you need me to come along?*

Me: *No. I will send the driver back for you, and he can deliver you to your hotel room when you're ready.*

Jax: thumbs up emoji

Next, I texted my driver and told him where to pick me up. Scooping up Isabelle, I headed for the back door, doing my best not to wake her. Whatever had caused her to faint was not medical; it was emotional and happened when a person needed to protect themselves. Unconsciousness could be a good thing. I entered the car with Isabelle in my arms, and John, my night driver, closed it behind us. Looking out the window as he pulled out, I saw Devi in the doorway we'd just vacated. I saw the question in her eyes.

I would text her later when I had time. I was still puzzled by her and Isabelle's introduction meeting earlier. Devi knew that Isabelle would be there as my date. Why had she acted so possessive of me? She'd never done that before.

Isabelle's response was stellar, so direct and powerful. I saw the goddess in her ability to exert self-control and express herself clearly and with purpose. I had not been offended in the least, and the interaction between the two of them had provoked Isabelle to say out loud that I was her boyfriend. That boded well for me; now to figure out what had been the cause of her passing out.

When we arrived at the penthouse garage, John opened my door and called the elevator for me. I sent him back to the party for Jax. Upstairs, I placed Isabelle on the couch and poured her a glass of water. I clapped my hands. To human ears, it would have sounded like a loud clap of the hands. To those of us born to immortality, it would have boomed like thunder.

Isabelle's eyes flew open. She sat up very suddenly, her eyes darting. "Bella, you're okay; we are in my penthouse, safe, where nothing can harm you. Please, drink some water." I held up the glass to her lips, and she drank greedily until the contents were gone and lay back as if exhausted by the simple task.

She gazed at me from her prone position, a silent tear sliding down from the corner of her eye. "I saw him, Iver. He was there, watching me from outside the window."

There could only be one *he*. I pulled Isabelle to me and held her tight as the waterworks released. Comforting her was my main priority, but after, I needed to get some security in place for her protection. Her worst nightmare had reappeared in her life. I wondered, was this Robert Voss immortal? Could he have known all along who she was and didn't bother killing her when she was a child because she was no threat then?

Had I attended alone, every fallen or descendant of a fallen would know who I was. Seeing her with me at the party could have made her a target to those less than savory fallen who wanted to end Ariella's lineage.

But how could he have possibly known she would be at that party? How did that monster manage to get on the guest list? More importantly, why now, why was he showing up now?

Isabelle's steady stream of tears had slowed down, and I felt her take a shuddering breath. That was a good sign. I leaned her back from my shoulder and looked into her beautiful, haunted eyes. "Tell me what happened." I used enough command in my voice to cut through any resistance she may have had.

"When I went to the bathroom, I was alone, so I texted Steve to tell him about my talk with Alan Partridge. I felt so happy, and I wanted to enjoy the feeling and run our conversation over in my head, to process everything. I went to the library, and when I found no one there, I wandered around, enjoying the place. I began to dream about my future and what I could do with my life and with my money if we got a contract with Alan's recording label."

Her eyes shone with her excitement. I could visualize her in the room, scanning the books, a small smile on her face as she let her imagination flow. It was at that moment that I saw another side of Isabelle, another place in which her unearthly beauty shone. Isabelle was so much more than a pretty face; her soul was stunning. Her humanity was more beautiful and radiant than anything I'd seen in thousands of years.

When her guard was down, it shone from her like an ethereal light. Being obnoxious and the Goth look she usually wore would have helped her hide. That is what she must have meant by feeling like she was pretending to be someone else when dressed in her gown.

She was so vulnerable, so exposed, how could I have missed that? I realized that the courtship was over. We would be together, and I would teach her how to protect herself. Beyond being given the mission by the archangel Michael, I was in love with her, and I would ensure her safety forever.

I was also furious. I told her *we* would go back to the library together. She had purposely gone on her own. I would need to ensure in the future that she heeded what I said. It was more important than I realized, as now the danger in her life was apparent. Some forces didn't want Ariella's child to live, and I would have to make sure she did.

"Anyway, it was when I was looking at an antique mirror that I caught sight of someone out of the corner of my eye. I didn't want whoever to know that I was aware of them. So, I continued around the room, looking at more books but watching from my peripheral vision. Then I saw the red again and then his face, and that's the last thing I remember."

I poured her more water. "Isabelle, before I get into other topics, I want to talk about your library visit. Didn't I tell you we would go back and check it out later, and I said I would show you mine as well?"

She looked away from me, her eyes looking anywhere but at mine. I knew she didn't like my tone. It reminded her of being at home with Jax, but I couldn't help it. I was toning down my fury so as not to scare her. But I wanted her a little bit scared. There would be consequences put in place for two reasons. One, I was a dominant and I needed to control, and two, her safety required it.

"Isabelle, look at me," I commanded. "I know you don't like this; my tone triggers your memories of being scolded by Jax."

She nodded, her eyes glassy with unshed tears.

"I am in love with you, Isabelle, and your safety is impor- tant to me, the most important thing to me. In a few short days, you have become everything, but moving forward, we are going to need some rules. It will all make sense to you when I explain more about who you are. But for now, this is just Iver the dominant, telling Isabelle the submissive that she will be receiving discipline if she does not keep her word, is that clear?"

She nodded her agreement.

"I need to hear you say it, Isabelle, acknowledge that you are submitting to my will in regard to your safety."

"Is there room for negotiation, or would being with you require that I have no choice?"

I sat back on the coffee table. My minx was recovering quickly from her earlier scare. For now, using our conversation as a diversion tactic was good. Still, I would have to be aware of this tactic and any others Isabelle may employ moving forward. If I allowed her to engage in it too frequently, she would come to rely on it and never dig for the truth or deeper meaning or consequences to her choices and actions.

"Let's lay it out. You have an old danger back in your life, and I won't rest until it's gone. Until then, your safety is up to me, but I can't do my job unless you allow it. That means I control your safety and implement security for you. Do you accept?"

"Well, of course, I agree, why wouldn't I? But I'm looking for the potential downside here."

I smiled at her, allowing Isabelle to see my dark self beneath the layers of good I usually projected. "Because, Isabelle, I am dominant, and if you don't do what I ask of you, there will be consequences, and the playful spankings that make you soaking wet will take on an entirely other meaning. Am I making myself clear?"

Even with the threat of a disciplinary spanking, Isabelle's arousal soared. Her submissive self craved direction and consequences. She had no idea how not sitting comfortably for a week would feel. But I had a feeling she would push and learn pretty quickly how mistaken she was to crave one.

I continued. "If I text you, unless you are playing on stage or in the recording studio, you will respond immediately. You will let me spoil you and cherish you. You will let me help you when you're down, frustrated, and in need. If I think a nap or a trip over my knee is going to give you the attitude adjustment you are asking me for through your actions, I will give it."

Again, her arousal spiked; she had a fantasy going about protection and correction. I hoped it would be all she needed it to be. Maybe I could dress like a cop, or a firefighter, or perhaps a principal. Have her bend over my desk in my office and administers strokes with a broad wooden ruler.

Now I was fantasizing, and I needed to stay on track. The fantasy stuff would be for playtime; this was serious.

"Do you understand?"

She licked her lips. "Yes," she husked.

And damn, if the bulge in my pants did not react to her. I held out my hand; safety protocols would have to wait until I released the ache in my balls. Right now, I needed to be inside her. She turned around for me so I could unzip her gown. It pooled at her feet, and she stood in only her heels and a bra.

"Isabelle, you are so delicious," I murmured in her ear, leaning her head back to rest against my shoulder. I ran both my hands down the front of her body, hiking up her bra. I fondled her beautiful, soft breasts, I flicked her pale pink rose-buds that quickly turned into stiffened peaks under my minis-trations. I thrummed her nipples as Isabelle emitted soft moans, arching into my hands. My left hand moved from one stiffened peak to the other. At the same time, my right hand slid down her side and wrapped around her hip, stroking the soft flesh between her thighs.

Her body trembled with the effort of standing in heels while I distracted her both on top and below. I swept her up and walked to the master bedroom. I laid her down and pulled off her heels as she reached behind herself and unclasped her bra.

I took off my suit jacket and my shirt and tie, leaving my pants to help support my raging hard-on. The little minx looked down at my cock and licked her lips again. "Come to the edge of the bed, Isabelle; turn around on all fours and lean down on your forearms." She did as she was told and her feet were dangling off the edge, her beautiful mound on full display, her engorged lips glistening in the soft light of the room.

I slid my belt off and folded it in half. I snapped it in the air, causing Isabelle to jump, and her beautiful folds release more of her fragrant juices. She was very excited. "Isabelle, you are not to orgasm without permission."

She nodded.

I snapped the belt across her backside. She yelped and turned her large green eyes in my direction.

"Words, please."

"Yes, Iver."

"Good girl, now turn around again and open your petals for me, Isabelle."

She moaned as she faced the headboard. I leaned on the ottoman at the end of the bed and began to alternate between licking her folds and flicking her sensitive nub. It was not long until she was bucking her hips.

She emitted the loveliest little mewls. My tongue was driving her over the edge, and I could feel her fighting to hold back her orgasm. I stopped licking and grabbed my belt—time for a different sensation. I began delivering soft smacks, alternating between her two cheeks.

At first, she protested and gave me an evil stare. I smacked the bottom of her cheeks, and she squealed, turning back around to face away from me, submitting to the light sensation spanking I was delivering.

Soon her lovely ass was bouncing to the rhythm of my belt, in anticipation of the next stroke. I stopped and plunged two digits into her wet folds. She orgasmed instantly, my wicked little minx; she needed better control.

I pulled out my digits and picked up my belt again. "Control yourself, Bella," I said as I swung the belt. These strokes were harder but far from being a punishment. Her ass jiggled as she tried avoiding the stinging swats.

I stopped and licked her juicy entrance. She sighed and pressed back into my mouth. I held her hips steady and went to town, licking and nipping her bud. I felt her trying to hold back another orgasm, and she was quivering with the struggle.

"Now, Isabelle."

She let go in a gush of juices as she shrieked her orgasm, her body peaking and crashing several times. I pulled down my pants and boxers and kicked out of my shoes at the same time. Aligning with her entrance, I plunged into her. I held still for a moment and then started to pull out to the tip and dive back in. Reaching around her ribs, I tweaked her nipples. "You can let go now, Isabelle, no more permission required."

Given the green light, Isabelle rocked back against me with a ferocity I didn't know she possessed. I felt her building to her next release. I continued to use one hand to tweak and gently pinch her nipples, while the other stabled her in place as I worked her inside the sheath. She was moaning and emitting the most beautiful sounds.

I felt her release. Her walls were squeezing me hard and milking me as I released inside of her. I was pumping her full of my semen. I opened myself up to her, allowed her to see my immortality when my seed spilled into her for the first time. She would see visions, she would know what I was and, better still, what she was.

She screamed her release again. I loved how sexual she was and unashamed of it. This time, with our mutual orgasms and no condom to block my seed, Isabelle would fall into a state of super consciousness that exists in a living dream realm. An alternate knowledge that belongs to the immortals, and she would see existence from heaven. She would witness the fall and her birth; she would see it all.

Chapter 17

Jax

The bevy of beauties, intellect, and money represented in the room was a marvel. I would have to thank Iver later. For the first time in forever, I felt like thanking my sister as well. Not that she was responsible for her parenting or her ancestry, but I was certainly benefiting from it.

I took my time moving around the grand entryway. The mansion, I'd heard of, as many critical events had taken place in these walls. Oh, if only to be a bug on the wall and tap into those Wall Street circles and secrets, I would be a happy man.

As I neared the grand staircase, I spotted a Wall Street shark, one of my idols, Jimmy Simpson, a hedge fund manager whose worth was estimated to be in the billions. Although not the richest man, he was definitely in the top fifty.

Surrounding him, was a group of young, vibrant, undergrad students from Harvard who looked like they were hanging on every word he spoke. Standing at his side, was a gorgeous, petite blonde. I stood apart, close enough to hear the conversation and far enough to not get caught staring at the blonde.

She looked up and smiled at me. I smiled back and shuffled a little closer to the circle, listening intently to the conversation in hopes of including myself. Simpson's flagship company, Medallion, was soon to be offering a new investment portfolio to its investors. With their program offering a sixty six percent return, they were the highest on investment returns trading on Wall Street.

Simpson was discussing the math behind their newest product and why he felt it would be revolutionary. The under-grads were doing their best to keep up to Jimmy's quantum explanation of the science.

"To summarize, you are saying that you can use your extra-large computer that allows your team of highly educated super brains to process large amounts of data. And that gives you *the edge* that all your other competitors are missing?"

Jimmy turned his head to see the person who went with the voice. He sized me up and down, and I guess I met with his seal of approval. He parted the crowd and reached out his hand. "Jimmy Simpson, and this is my granddaughter, Lillith."

Granddaughter, thank you, Lord, I uttered a prayer. Reaching out my hand in return, I introduced myself, "Jaxon Ackles, Jax for short, please. I'm delighted to meet you, sir."

I was grateful, but it was hard to take my eyes off Lillith. She looked like a sexy little cherub, which, up until this moment, I had no idea was my taste.

"What business are you in, son?"

"Acquisitions and mergers," I said, pulling my eyes from Lillith to Jimmy. "But I am interested in everything, and I am here tonight in hopes of spreading my wings, or at the very least to meet beautiful people." My eyes had wandered back to Lillith. Realizing what I'd just said, I added, "I mean great people whom I can connect with, sir."

Jimmy chuckled. "That's fine, my boy, meeting a beautiful young woman can have that effect on a man. Why don't you join Lillith and me for a drink before dinner and tell us more about what you do and where you want to direct your investments. Maybe I can be of help?"

Taking his hand, I shook it. "I am honored, sir, thank you kindly." With that, I left the gathering and made my way through the crowd of the rich and wealthy. I was trying to think of what I would do or say to impress the man, when I caught sight of Iver escorting my sister away from the room and down a hallway, no doubt looking for some privacy.

I didn't envy Iver; my sister was probably acting like a brat. I laughed inwardly, not my problem. Iver had made it very clear that Issy was hands-off. I wished them luck and continued my journey around the room, passing the famous rapper Jacob Rea.

Stopping to look at the eclectic display of art on the walls, I managed to gain access to conversations regarding up and coming artists whose work was going for a steal and would triple in value in less than a year. Good tip, I would have to purchase a piece or two before I left the party.

Occasionally, I caught glances of Lillith and her grandfather, Jimmy. She would be all smiles with whomever they were standing with, but she didn't speak. Better to hold back commenting on things one didn't have the proclivities to discuss with authority. I assumed she must be bored to tears.

She caught me gaping at her a few times and winked in my direction, her cherub looks instantly transforming to the ultimate seductress. I felt myself get hard in my pants. How could this group of people not be falling all over themselves to get to her? She was gorgeous and outshone every other woman in the room by a long shot.

When it was time to meet up with them, I sauntered into the sitting room, expecting a crowd to contend with; instead, I was pleasantly surprised when I found I was the only guest. Lillith gave me a smile that I felt down to my crotch.

The vixen, did she know that she was giving me a case of the worst blue balls I'd ever had? Jimmy smiled, standing up and taking my hand. "Sit down, Mr. Ackles."

"Please, call me Jax."

He smiled. "Only if you return the favor and call me Jimmy."

Once we were seated and champagne flutes served, we chitchatted about the event. "Who extended you an invitation to this private event, Jax, maybe I know them?" Jimmy spoke.

I sat back; this was my trump card, and I wanted to milk it. "You may; my sister's boyfriend, Iver Eriskay." Lillith, who was sipping her champagne, choked. I quickly grabbed her a bottle of water from a server walking by. When she stopped coughing, she looked at me and said, "You are Isabelle's brother?"

It was my turn to sputter, "You know Isabelle?"

She looked uncomfortable. "Well, yes. I work for one of Iver's companies. Isabelle and I met earlier today."

I put two and two together. "You work at the spa?"

She blushed and nodded. Jimmy said, "I don't know why she wastes her time and talent. I have asked Lillith to come and work for me dozens of times; she would make ten times the amount she makes at the spa."

"I told you, Grandpa," Lillith answered. "I like having the time to do what I want." She said the word *want* while she looked directly at me. My cock sprang to attention again. *Damn woman.* I crossed my legs to hide her effect on me.

"When I'm ready to settle down and move on to the next stage in my life, I will come work for you. In the meantime, I work whatever hours I want, and my time off is my own." Again, she glanced at me—the word *own* hanging between us. I got the distinct feeling that if I got into bed with this girl, I would never get out. For some reason, that didn't cause me to panic as it usually did.

Instead, I couldn't help having visions of us in a home,

maybe the upper east side, with two beautiful children. Our daughter would be talented and have the angel face of her mother. While our son would look like me and be like his mother, he would be an artist and maybe even go to Juilliard.

I shook my head, what the? Was I fantasizing, or having a vision? Lillith smiled like a kitty that had eaten a treasured canary. Did she make me see that? I suddenly felt way out of my league. We were called to dinner, and despite not having gotten to discuss business with Jimmy, I was ready for a respite from the tantalizing Lillith.

I was surprised when seated for dinner that I was beside her and her dear grandfather, sandwiched in with the Harvard undergrads. It was a perfect seating arrangement for him, as he seemed to love the attention they were lavishing on him.

Once the first course was served, and Lillith and I were left alone. I asked her, "Did you make the seating arrangements?"

She smiled. "Let us just say that a friend of mine is the coordinator. I had her revamp a few seats before everyone entered the dining room. Do you mind?"

"Not in the least, I find myself in the company of the most beautiful woman I have ever laid eyes on, how could I possibly mind?"

She slid her hand to my lap and placed it directly on top of my raging hard-on. "I'm glad you feel that way. I like you too," she answered almost shyly.

"Do you want to get out of here?" she asked me after our dishes were removed and the second course was served.

The ball was back in my court. Did I want a premature exit? Not really, I still had people to mill through. "What's the rush, beautiful? Why not get our fill, the night is still young, and what about dessert?"

She leaned into me, rubbing my crotch. "I have a different dessert in mind," she whispered. I inhaled her scent; she was a blend of rose oil and heather, a fascinating combination. "Lillith," I said, grasping her hand and removing it from my bulge. "Where are you from, your ancestry, I mean."

"Scotland, but our family has been here for over one hundred years. How about you?"

"Honestly, I'm not sure. At some point a long time ago, we migrated from the middle east but have been part of the American culture since its birth pretty much."

She examined my features. "You don't look middle eastern; it must have been a long time ago."

"As I said, my family has been in America for over three hundred years. We are American. Before that doesn't matter, does it?"

She shook her head. "The only thing that matters to me right now is spending time with you, alone."

She looked young; I used the last of my resistance to ask her age. I wasn't interested in being a sugar daddy to anyone despite the attraction I felt for her. "How old are you, Lillith?"

She blushed. "Old enough," was her answer.

I gazed down my nose at her and did my best intimidation stare. One I would have given to Issy when she was younger and wanted the truth from her about what she'd been doing.

She sighed. "I'm twenty-three, and you?"

I sighed in relief. "Thirty-four, are you sure you want to go home with an old man?" I was kidding, well, sort of. I genuinely needed to know what she thought of our age difference."

"Yes," she husked, "I genuinely do."

With dinner done, we were going to make our escape; she waltzed over to her grandfather to say she was going home early, when I received a text from Iver. Issy had fainted, and he was taking her back to his place and would be sending the limo back for us. I ensured he didn't need me and went to meet Lillith in the gardens, where we kissed until the limo showed up to take us to my hotel for the night.

Chapter 18

Lillith

What were the chances that I would meet both Ackles in one day? Well, two Ackles, Jax told me about his younger brother, Finn, over dinner.

When Jax walked toward our group, where I stood with my grandfather, I felt an instant attraction. He was tall, gorgeous, and wore a permanent smirk on his face somewhere between cocky and pissed off.

Then, when he smiled, his entire face lit up and illuminated him from the inside out. He was a puzzle who I wished to know better. I noticed that although he spoke with my grandfather, as had been his mission, Jax had eyes only for me.

I know I have a sexy cherub, seductress vibe that attracted older men like flies to honey. I had used my looks to my advantage when I was attracted to someone.

There was something different about Jax Ackles that I couldn't put my finger on. Why, in a room full of good-looking people, did he stand out like a beacon of light? I can't say for sure, but beyond the mutual attraction, there was something more, like a yearning or a pull.

There was an ancient Sumerian saying that *when one is committed, the other half would come forth and be recognized.* My interpretation of that meant when I was ready, I would get a hook up with an immortal, and we would live our eternal life together forever. I needed to have a bird and the bees talk with Iver.

I suspected that Jax might be a descendant of the fallen, and I wanted to know how the immortal thing worked. Before my time, a mighty angel fell and mated with a demigod; a precious lineage was born that was now in danger.

If that happened, then immortality would be gone from this earth, and we immortals would all lose our immortal genes. I made a note in my phone schedule to talk to Iver. I needed to know what the scoop was and if I should be waiting for some superman to walk into my life. Because I kind of feel like one just did, and if I am right, and he is immortal, how do I activate his dormant genes?

Chapter 19

Isabelle

I woke up to the sun shining through the blinds of Iver's lavish penthouse bedroom. I rolled over with a groan. Last night had been amazing, but I was a little sore from all the sex. I wasn't used to it. Blinking open an eye, I found a steaming cup of coffee mocha on the nightstand. I folded up to sitting and leaned my back against the headboard, gazing out to the city, with my coffee in hand.

Had I become a spoilt, kept woman in an ivory tower already? I sighed and let my mind travel to last night. The evening had been strange, to say the least. First, meeting that Devi girl and then Robert Voss showing up and watching me. An involuntary shudder ran through me, thinking about that creep watching me.

"Good morning, goddess."

I hadn't noticed Iver sitting in the chair on the other side of the room, too preoccupied with waking up. He'd been watching me, but unlike the creepy vibe that Robert gave off, having Iver watching over me felt good.

"Good morning back," I answered.

He moved to the bed and sat on the end opposite me, so I had no choice but to gaze at his perfect mug. His eyes were glittering in the morning light. He was so gorgeous; I felt my nipples peak just looking at him. The soreness I'd felt when I woke up suddenly disappeared.

I stared at him unabashed, not having bothered to cover my upper half with the blanket. We had a staring match, and I wondered what was on his mind. Probably the safety thing. We never got around to that conversation, other than me agreeing to let him be my protector.

"Your assistant is creepy." I broke the silent eye battle with my blunt statement.

And it had the effect I wanted as Iver's steely gaze lightened and he erupted into laughter. "You are something, Bella; you know that?"

I smirked, "So I've been told." I put my mug down and looked at him. "All kidding aside, Iver, there is something wrong with that girl."

He sat back, looking smug. "Why, because Devi shows an unnatural fondness for her boss? She probably has a Fifty Shades fetish. I mean, I am the ultimate Dom, don't you think?"

I knew he was playing because of the big grin he wore, but that also meant he wasn't taking what I said seriously. I needed him to understand. "Iver, my necklace, where did you get it? I mean, do you know what it is?"

His face took on a thoughtful expression; he unfolded his legs and came closer. His gift still hung around my neck. I could feel it like it had a life of its own. Iver slid his hand underneath the amulet and gave it a full examination, front and back.

"It is Sumerian," he said, looking up at me. "But you knew that already, didn't you, Isabelle?"

He slid his hand away and sat back, examining me. I felt like he could read my soul, that I would be weighed and judged like Anubis victims as they headed through the gates of the underworld. "I only know it's old, and the markings remind me of the one I showed you at dinner the other night, the one that has passed down the female family line. The one thing my mother left for me before she died. Jax gave it to me on my sixteenth birthday."

"Isabelle, we need to talk about your mother, well, about your family ancestry and me and how we linked up. It wasn't accidental."

I eyed him and thought back to my vivid dreams during the night. I chalked them up to post-coital bliss, but maybe it had been more than that. What I had dreamt about seemed crazy, yet looking at Iver, he could be that guy from my dream.

I'd seen a man who looked exactly like Iver at the end of the bronze age. I saw him in an African jungle, and I saw him fighting in a massive battle in Egypt, with an ankh similar to the one on my necklace, in a circlet around his head. Iver's lookalike was in the mountains, in a Buddhist temple, sailing in an ancient ship that looked like it was easily a thousand years old. Iver's lookalike existed in every age in history.

Iver watched me intently.

"They weren't dreams, were they? Who are you, Iver? And, more importantly, who the hell am I?" I was trembling. Somehow, I knew that whatever Iver was going to tell me would forever change my life, and I was scared.

He sidled up to me and took my hands in his. "Isabelle Ackles, you are the savior. The savior of the fallen, the savior of angels and demons and their offspring. You are the savior, Isabelle, and I am your protector and fated mate."

I didn't know what I had been expecting, but that wasn't it. I started laughing, just small at first, but my laugh quickly grew into full wracking laughter that I couldn't control.

"Isabelle, stop!"

I did, instantly. That was the second time Iver had issued a command I felt compelled to follow.

"Iver, do you have control over me? Can you make me do things?"

He nodded. "I can, but I would prefer to have you decide than to control you. When you can't, like just then, I will take over. You are only twenty years old, Isabelle. I may look only twenty-five years old, but I am one of the oldest beings on this planet. Our kind is dying out, and with a new threat, we are in danger. Only you can save us, Isabelle."

Chapter 20

Iver

She turned her gaze away from me and out the window. I knew she no longer saw the city from her former lenses. Her world had just blown to pieces. Her next question surprised me. "How many fell, and how many are left?"

I sighed, "Honestly, I don't know. My father, Enoch, tells me that fifteen hundred were tossed out of Heaven, for various reasons. They were scattered as they fell, no two in the same place. Alone and fearful, most, like my father, went into hiding. While others amalgamated into some form of civilization, the children of the immortals should have been activated and become immortal themselves. But if left ignorant, they lived a mortal life and, like all humans, eventually died. Enoch was a senior angel, God's scribe. He had access to information that few in the heavenly realms had access to, only God, Michael, and himself. He is still unclear as to why he was in the group of fallen."

I stopped for a minute to let what I said soak in. "The

church says that the fallen came to Earth and became demons through their greed. That is just a story, a euphemism to subjugate would be sinners. Half of the heavenly host were warriors and don't possess an evil bone in their bodies. But there are rumors of a group of the fallen that created the downfall of specific angels to weaken Heaven. Stuck in human forms, the angels can do nothing to help heavenly realms if there is a celestial battle. On Earth, we can fight for humanity; we can try to right some wrongs created by humans that are driven by greed and wealth. Sorry, I have gotten carried away. My father believes there are only five hundred or so left of the original, and of the offspring, hard to say. As I said, many of them have no idea what they are. You mentioned Devi; she is a descendant from the same line as your brothers, and her immortality was activated by me."

Isabelle gave me a penetrating look. "She is not one of us, Iver, and she is dangerous. I have always been able to sense people's intentions. Hers are self-serving; she recognized my necklace. You saw her touch it. What you don't know is that it burned her. She pulled away so quickly, because my ankh, the one you gave me, didn't like her. I realize that sounds crazy, but it's true. And what do you mean by Devi descending from the same lineage as my brothers? What about me?"

I blew out a breath. *Here we go.* "Isabelle, you were born of an angel and a god. Your mother, Ariella, was one of the originals, a seraphim. She became a warrior queen on Earth, around four thousand years ago. She had a baby with the Roman god, Apollo. Every thousand years, she gives birth, to keep her lineage intact. Ariella wasn't like the other immortals; she carried the ability, like my father, to pass on the direct genes with no activation required. But to keep you safe, like your three sisters, she placed you in a family of her lineage but not direct descendants, your immortality covered in a veil. That is why you have had no inkling as to who you are or of your special powers. My father says that the daughter of Apollo and Ariella, born every thousand years, is who keeps the fallen's divine qualities from fading."

Isabelle seemed genuinely concerned. "I have sisters? Where are they?"

I squeezed her hand. Although she had never met her full-blooded sisters, to learn of their existence and to lose them in the same conversation would be hard. "They are dead, Isabelle. Someone doesn't want the heavenly hosts here on Earth to live. Hellfire is a sure way to kill off immortals. But here is the kicker; even my father didn't know that hellfire could do that. Michael came down and told us when he gave me the job to find and protect you."

She was glaring at me, not the reaction I expected. "Okay, so let me get this straight. I have sisters, sorry, had sisters, and some sinister shit head has wiped them out? My brothers aren't my brothers, and you have been sent by an archangel to protect me?"

She erupted into laughter. Like earlier, laughing so hard, she began to cry. "Why not just say you are a vampire; that would have been more realistic than this crazy story," she gasped out.

Her brain was on overload. She needed to touch down on Earth, connect with things that were here and now. I pulled her over my lap, wrapping my leg over both of hers and started smacking her naked ass. Within seconds, the desired effect happened, and she was in her body, feeling the heat building in her perfect cheeks.

I sat her back up; she glared at me but said nothing as she quickly rolled onto her side, rubbing her flaming cheeks. I looked into her eyes. "I will look into Devi. I haven't known the family for long, but I will find out if they have nefarious intentions toward you."

She sighed with relief. Keeping the conversation to something she could handle was important. She was still just a twenty-year-old woman, living her life. She would, in time, learn how to navigate the waters of eternity.

I didn't say anything to her, but the necklace incident was disturbing. My gut told me Devi couldn't be trusted. My thoughts drifted to Robert Voss outside the window of the room Isabelle was checking. How would he even know where to look? How would he know to look through that window? There had to be someone else he was in league with him, and I hoped it wasn't Devi.

"We need to get you moved in here today, get you a burner phone, check all your clothing for bugs. Let's leave everything in your apartment and get you everything new on this end. Less work, then we will iron out a security detail, and we need to shut down any social media."

Isabelle rose from the bed. "Really, Iver, you're just going to take over?"

My arms crossed my chest. "Yes, Isabelle, this is what I do, and you already agreed to this, last night."

She swirled around and pointed her finger in my face. "I need social media. I have a career, and the savior or not, I plan on rising to the top in my career. Don't even think about stopping me."

I grabbed her hand and resisted the urge to pull her over my lap again, showing what happens to rude goddesses. But instead, I drew her fingers to my lips and kissed every one of them. "Isabelle, we can talk and work through anything. All you need to do is convey the importance of each item. I'm not here to control you, I'm here to keep you safe, but if you fight me on this, our fun times won't be nearly as pleasant. Do you want to spend the next hundred years tied to my bed?" I was only half-serious, to distract her from the potential negative side to this conversation. I slowly slid each of her fingers into my mouth, one at a time.

By the time I got to her pinkie on her second hand, she was moaning. I pushed her gently back onto the bed and, lifting her knees, brought my tongue down to her slick entrance. She was ready for me. I delved my tongue and parted her swollen lips, licking and nibbling her sore private bits.

Her hips writhed under my ministrations. "Please, Iver," she begged, "I need you inside of me."

I stood and dropped my pants. "As you wish, my little goddess." I plunged into her, igniting an earth-shattering scream. She'd gone primal, bucking and writhing like an animal as I took her hard and fast. We weren't making love; we were two primal beings coupling. I could almost envision us in the plains of Africa, rutting among the other predators. For some reason, this image incited me, and I plunged deeper, claiming every inch of her body for myself. *Mine,* I told myself, *mine and no other's, ever.*

When I knew she could hold on no longer, I shouted, "Now!" and Isabelle and I both exploded on my command as we slowed down and gently fell back to Earth. I moved onto the bed and pulled her back against my torso.

"I love you, Isabelle, I love you, and I promise to keep you safe."

She pressed her warm ass into my groin and sighed. She slipped off into slumber, and I held her tightly. If only I could do this forever, never leave the sanctuary of my apartment or even this bed, just be entwined in ecstasy for the next thousand years.

Chapter 21

Isabelle

The move was quick and uneventful; I grabbed a suitcase worth of stuff, and Iver thoroughly searched the contents to ensure there were no bugs or tracking devices. Now safely ensconced in Iver's ivory tower, I got ready for my meeting with the guys and Alan Partridge.

Iver offered to escort me, but I didn't want to show up at the studio with my *boyfriend*, no matter how gorgeous and powerful he was. Besides, in the short week since we'd met, my entire life had changed. I wanted to see Steve and Marshall; hopefully, they were unchanged, and I could connect with my old life.

That was a bit of a lark. My old life was small, and most of it I had spent in hiding. But it had been entirely mine, and now I was grieving my old self, simply because I was no longer her. I wondered if the changes I felt so profoundly were evident on the outside.

I studied myself in the palatial bathroom mirror. I felt ten years older, but age-wise, I looked the same. But something had changed. What was it?

Iver walked into the bathroom. Glancing at me, he said, "You look softer."

I stared at him in the mirror. "Can you read minds, or just mine?"

He laughed. "I can read a lot, but not minds, more like desires and intentions, not thoughts. You are examining yourself as if your life depends on it. So, you are looking to see if you can see your immortality, if you appear older, if all the riotous emotions you are feeling are evident from the outside. The answer is you look softer; love can do that to a person. You also seem more comfortable in your skin, and if possible, those two things have added to your already gorgeous, goddess appearance. You look like a queen, Isabelle, my queen."

I smirked in the mirror. "Well, your queen wishes she had time to let you bow at her feet and provide her with untold pleasures, but she has a date with destiny."

He stood behind me now. Grabbing both my ass cheeks in his hands, he roughly gripped and massaged them, his eyes trained on mine. "I thought I was your destiny. Isn't that what you were shouting out amid your multiple orgasms?" He leaned down and nipped my ear.

Now it was my turn to laugh. "You are incorrigible, you know that. I gotta go."

He released my ass cheeks and followed me to the front door. He was dropping me off, and a driver would pick me up and bring me back when I was ready. We both agreed that having security inside seemed pointless as we weren't sure if anyone was aware of my ancestry at this time. My mother had gone to some lengths to keep my identity hidden, and so had my adoptive parents. It seemed so weird to say that—*my adoptive parents*. I had a lot of adapting to do. Anyway, despite any potential threats, currently, mine seemed quite human, and hellfire bombs were not a concern.

Iver distributed Robert Voss' picture to his security team and those at Alan's studio. Iver didn't want anyone sneaking in who didn't belong.

He was driving the Mercedes today. I discovered that Iver had a private garage that housed a dozen exotic and domestic vehicles. He owned the building we're living in, and when he had it built, he reserved the top floor for himself, with built-in conveniences, like his private elevator and a personal parking area within the garage.

"Iver, how exactly do you know Alan Partridge? I assumed it was through the Renaissance Ball, but do you have business with him outside of the events?"

"I do know Alan outside of the Renaissance Ball. He is excited about talking to you and asked to do the reveal regarding the nature of our friendship. I don't want to ruin it for him."

I rolled my eyes. *Whatever.* "Thanks, lover, for sending me into the lion's den with no ammunition."

He pulled up outside of Prism Studios, Alan's recording empire. "Have fun, my love; be safe, and don't forget, answer my messages."

I nodded and exited the car. He waited until I was inside the building and had joined Marshall and Steve, before pulling out into traffic. It was our first time apart for any length of time, and I felt strangely bereft.

I texted him.

Me: *I miss you already*
    Iver: *I miss you too, be good.*
    Me: tongue out emoji

Iver: laughy face emoji *or else* spanking emoji
Me: rolling eyes emoji

Tucking my phone into my pocket, I gave Marshall and Steve a hug. "I missed you guys. It's only been a week, but it feels like a month or more."

They both examined me, both wearing identical looks, curiosity. Finally, Steve broke the silence, "So how did you arrange this meeting, and who was the guy in the car? It looked like Iver."

I grinned as I told them, "It *was* Iver; he's my bitch. Now let's go, or we'll be late."

My answer had the desired effect; both guys laughed, and the tension I'd been feeling disappeared. We arrived at reception and were greeted by name, by the super-hot girl who ran his front line of defense. "Mr. Partridge is ready to see you," she said, coming around and shaking hands with me and then Steve.

Marshall, who had always remained unaffected by females, stood gawking. The woman, Elsa, grinned and held out her hand to him. "It's nice to meet you. I heard that you are quite a talent. Maybe you can show me sometime, your talent that is."

Wow, right out of the gate, Marshall was receiving some intense attention. Unused to it, I expected him to start rambling or go silent with that deer in the headlights look he often had when the opposite gender noticed him.

Not this time, much to the surprise of Steve and me. Marshall lifted her hand to his lips and kissed the back. "Showing you my talent is an absolute must, shall we say this evening at 7:00? I can pick you up?"

Steve and I exchanged looks of shock. I guess I wasn't the only one to change in the time we'd been apart. As we walked down the hall, we trailed behind Elsa and Marshall, allowing them some privacy. "You may as well confess now," I said to Steve.

"Confess to what, exactly?"

"I don't know, like what happened to you in the last few days. Did you meet the love of your life, or go through a personality transformation? Marshall and I can't be the only ones, so what's yours?"

Steve was usually pretty upfront, Marshall was the closed-off one, but for some reason, they seemed to have traded roles. Steve hunched his shoulders like he had nothing to offer. I let it go. Whatever had changed for him, he wasn't about to share it with me.

I shifted my attention to the building; it was mammoth on the inside. I had no idea it housed so much equipment and staging. We stopped at a vast room, set up as a small concert hall and filled with studio equipment.

"This is the room we use for artists with no recording background," Elsa explained. "Our idea in putting it together is to give bands the same vibe as a small venue would provide, so they are more comfortable with the early stages of their recording careers. Here, they have the space to play without too much pressure. If anything of value comes of it, the recordings are stored and then shared in a superior sound booth."

As the band's sound would be its brand, unlike business artists whose brands were their style, and finding and perfecting their *technique,* is what made the difference between mediocre success and success on a grand scale.

I admitted to myself that I had never really spent a lot of time identifying where we fit in the spectrum. I had always left that up to Steve and Marshall. But with all the changes this past week, I found I had space and capacity to have an interest beyond just playing the drums. I wanted to know how it all worked.

We continued down another series of hallways, finally stopping outside of Alan's office. Despite having met him, I found myself nervous; my palms were sweaty. Quickly wiping them down my new designer jeans that Iver had bought me, I shook off my nervousness and plastered a smile on my face.

"Come in," he said when Elsa knocked. She opened the door, and my megawatt smile faltered. Alan wasn't the only one in the room; there was also the head singer, Vaughn, for the band RIP, Steve's all-time hero. Megan Merk, from the dirty girl's band Funk, and Jonas Foster, by far the biggest talent in sound for all the mega movie soundtracks.

We were standing in the doorway, feeling severely outclassed. I stood, frozen, what the? Steve and Marshall were beside me looking like alabaster statues, they'd paled so much. I thought back to my conversation in the car with Iver. He knew, the asshole; I was going to give him a piece of my mind when I saw him later tonight.

I swallowed and spoke up. "Alan, it is so good of you to make time for us, but clearly, you are busy, we can reschedule for later in the week." I started backing up, and the guys followed me, when Alan stood up.

He was laughing as he walked around his desk, making the introductions, "Don't be silly, Vaughn, Megan, and Jonas are partners with me on many of my endeavors. I invited them here to meet you. When we spoke at the ball, Isabelle, and you shared who your musical heroes were, I didn't want to spoil our conversation by saying that you could meet and work with your peers."

I was shocked, and so were the guys. Neither of them had uttered a word, and they looked like wooden puppets when they shook hands with the musicians. "But, Alan, you don't even know if we're any good yet. Why would you pull in the big guns?" I asked, looking around the room. "You haven't even auditioned us yet?"

Alan leaned back on his desk, and the four of them all wore grins. They knew something we didn't. "I don't mean to sound cocky." He laughed. "Okay, maybe I do. I have heard several of your songs."

We three looked at each other in confusion, and then it hit me. "Iver and Raphe, they must have recorded us at the club when they came to check us out. Raphe did say that many of today's biggest names got started at Swank."

Alan grinned and nodded his head. "You are correct, Isabelle. What you don't know is I own that club, with Raphe and Iver."

Damn you, Iver, I silently cursed him. He could have told me that. He probably had a hidden camera in here so he could watch the shock on my face. I was angry enough with Iver to become comfortable with my surroundings. "So, you have heard us, and now what, you want to work with us, or is this just some game that Iver has set up with you?"

Alan regarded me. I, in turn, eyed him with the full impact of my inner goddess. I wasn't letting him pull all the punches. Damn them all if I looked like an ignorant girl.

Alan smirked, "Iver is right; you are quite a force. Your equipment is all set; we thought you guys could jam, play a few pieces, and then we could discuss your future."

When we finished at the studio, it was almost evening. Exiting out the studio doors, hand in hand, the guys and I had a victory shout. The day had been fantastic, better than any dreaming I'd done could have been. We left with a contract in hand. Our days of playing dark little clubs were over.

The three of us hugged. We said our goodbyes, and I headed to Iver's car. His driver wasn't Benson; it was someone else who looked vaguely familiar. I reached into my pocket for my cell phone to text Iver about his driver when I was grabbed and thrown into the car. I scrambled for the handle of the door to get out when a rag went over my mouth and nose. I fought until I succumbed to the darkness.

Chapter 22

Iver

I couldn't help chuckling during the drive to my office. I wish I could have been there to see Isabelle's face when she found out that I was in business with Alan and the rest of her musical heroes.

I pulled into my parking garage and texted Benson, letting him know to pick Isabelle up at 5:30 from the studio and bring her back to the penthouse. Then I went into my office on the 56th floor and started my day.

I had diverted as much work as I could, and today was catch up day. Despite my full schedule, I made sure to check in with Isabelle, and she kept her agreement to keep me in the loop.

I had felt her hesitancy in the car. We'd had an intense week together, and today was our first full day apart. I'd learned this week that Isabelle was a walking contradiction in so many ways, more than she could see. It wasn't her fault, living with no parents and two brothers, one of whom had let her down repeatedly. That had created some bad habits in my newly made goddess that I intended to rectify.

Now that she knew who she was and her importance to our kind, with her warrior in place—me—to keep her safe, Isabelle could grow into the person she was meant to be and not a walking contraction of personality traits and emotions. I was looking forward to an eternity of learning about her and helping her remove her wrapping.

At 5:30, I received a text from Benson saying he had arrived at the studio and was waiting for Isabelle. My phone pinged a few minutes later. Assuming it was Isabelle, I opened the text message.

It was a picture of Isabelle, passed out on a back seat, her mouth covered and her arms tied behind her back and the caption '*I win, asshole*' printed on it.

I felt the world spin out of control. I called Benson, no answer. He probably wasn't the one who had been texting me; someone else had gotten hold of his phone.

I called the head of my security detail. "John, I need you to find Benson."

John paused. "He is picking up Isabelle."

"No, John, he isn't. Someone else took the car and picked up Isabelle, and now she is in grave danger. Also, get a hold of Alan, I need video footage from out front of the studio. You know what? Tell him to get it ready; I'm heading there now. Also, get a hold of Richard and tell him to run a trace on Isabelle's phone."

"Right, boss, anything else?"

"Let's get these steps done first, then we'll see what else needs to happen. We need to find her sooner rather than later. The guy who took her, the one in the photo I had you distribute to our men, is crazy, and I don't know what his plans are for her."

I hung up the phone and walked on unsteady legs to the elevators. As I rounded the corner, I caught sight of Devi. She saw me and quickly headed back the way she came. *Odd behavior*, I thought, and then I remembered what Isabelle had said about Devi. She didn't trust her. Could she have been the one to tell Robert what room she was in at the Renaissance Ball?

"Devi," I called, "hold up."

She stopped dead in her tracks. She seemed edgy, and when I looked into her eyes, I saw it. She knew something about Isabelle. I grabbed her by her upper arm and marched her into one of the empty offices.

I sat her down in a chair, not pleasantly, and said one word, "Spill."

She had recovered and was giving away nothing. "I'm sorry, Iver, I'm not sure what you mean?"

Had she always been deceptive, and I'd missed it? I admit to being too trusting of my fellow immortals and their kin, still giving them the benefit of the doubt. The ones who fell were not all good. Some of them had ulterior motives, and I was firsthand seeing one.

"Let me put it in words you will understand. Hellfire is not the only way to kill an immortal, once their recessive genes are activated. I can think of a dozen ways to kill you right here in this office. So, if you're fond of living, I suggest you confess right now."

During my little speech, her eyes had gone from closeted to fearful. I had lived through and witnessed the inquisition and many other times in history when humanity treated each other despicably.

"All I did was tell him she was there and let him know when she was alone."

The fury I had been holding back unleashed, and I know my eyes went red as my anger rose to heights I'd never felt before. "Why?" I roared.

She flinched and tried to bury herself in the back of her chair. I grabbed her hair and pulled her head back. "Why?" I uttered that one word, dripping with barely contained fury. "Tell me quickly, or I will snap your head from your body."

She eyed me as if I should know of her deception. "Isn't it obvious, Iver? I'm in love with you, and I wanted her gone."

I released her head, and it snapped back up. "Then, you know where he has taken her?"

Now she looked confused. "What do you mean by 'he's taken her'? He said he wanted to mess with her, and I thought when you saw all her baggage, you would drop her and pick me instead. When did he take her?"

I was wasting time, probably what he'd intended. I'd taken the time to find out how he'd known where Isabelle was, and that would take time away from finding her in time. "If she's dead, I will come back and finish you."

Tears filled her eyes. Disgusted, I walked out of the room and stopped to talk to Anne, my receptionist. "Have Devi's computer, phone, and any other devices taken. Make sure she leaves here with nothing and remove her ID tags. She will never be allowed in this building again."

Anne looked shocked but nodded her head. She knew better than to question me when I was angry, and right now I was seething. I'm sure she and the entire floor heard me yelling at Devi. I took the elevator down to my car and raced to the studio. As I did, a text came from John.

John: *I found Benson, his throat cut. Sorry, boss. His keys and phone were missing.*

Damn it!

Me: *Run a trace on Benson's phone, along with Isabelle's.*

John: *Did. Both are in the same location, about a mile from the studio. He ditched them.*

. . .

Damn! I hit the steering wheel with my fists. Where could he have taken her? I arrived at the studio; Alan was waiting for me with the footage from the outdoor cameras. I saw when Isabelle realized Benson wasn't driving and pulled out her phone, probably to text me as to the change in driver.

With her attention on her phone, the driver grabbed her and threw her into the back seat. As she tried to scramble out, someone from inside the car reached and pulled her in, sticking a cloth over her face, and within seconds she stopped struggling. The arm pulled back, and the person attached to the appendages made an appearance, confirming my fear.

Robert looked directly up at the camera with an evil grin on his face. The driver slammed the door, and they took off. I phoned John. "I should have thought of this already. Use your connections downtown and find out where Benson's car is heading. I just need a direction."

I hung up the phone. Alan placed his hands on my shoulders. "Stay tough, buddy, we will find her."

I stood up and suddenly felt my immortality weighing heavily on my shoulders. If Isabelle died, I would join her in death. I would have failed my mission and lost the only woman I'd ever loved.

I was climbing into my car when I had an idea. I phoned Jax.

"Hey, Iver, what's up?"

"Your sister, she has been kidnapped by Robert Voss."

"What? How?"

"It's a story we don't have time for right now, Jax. I need you to think. Robert wants to go back in time and finish what he started with Isabelle. Where would he go?"

"It would have to be our old neighborhood. The school, or

maybe his old house, or maybe mine. You take my old house, and I will go to Robert's, texting the address now."

I punched the address into my GPS. I was half an hour away.

"Jax, aren't you in Jersey? You're like two hours away; she could be dead by then."

"No, I'm in the city. I'll be there in about twenty minutes."

"I'm sending my team to the two locations; you will need back up. And, Jax, caution, please use your head; your sister's life is at stake."

I peeled out of the parking lot, quickly phoning John back with the plan. We should all converge in the general location at the same time, but I wanted to be the one to find her. I drove like a madman, arriving fifteen minutes later.

Benson's car was nowhere in sight, but I had a feeling. My gut said she was inside. I went into stealth mode, hiding from view and walking around the house. Peering in every window, I saw her tied down on a bed, facing the window where I stood, eyes closed.

I sent out a vibration to her, letting her know I was there. She opened one glassy eye; when she saw me, a single tear slid down her cheek. I held my finger to my lips in a gesture of remaining silent and pulled out my phone. I quickly texted the guys where I was and that Isabelle was in their old house.

I instructed John to break through the front door as I went through the back. I told him to set his timer, so the intrusion was simultaneous. Just as I left the window to move to the back door, Robert walked into the bedroom.

Isabelle's eyes grew round with terror, and she started pulling on the ropes that held her. Damn, plan B. I hurled myself through the window, rolled, and came up to stand just as the countdown finished.

Robert looked up in surprise, and I took advantage of his inertia and ripped his head clean off. I heard the front door crash, a scuffle, then silence. I was untying Isabelle when Jax, John, and two others from my security team came rushing in. I undid the last knot and then pulled her into my arms.

By now, her single tear had turned into a flood as she cried. I felt all the fear and remorse leave her body. Jax, ignoring the decapitated head on the floor, sat on her other side and placed his hands on her back so she would know he was with her.

I enfolded all of us in peace. I was using what was left of my strength to fill us all with peace, healing, and love. I felt Jax embrace the energy field I was emitting and lend his to it, confirming and activating his immortal genes.

John, when he'd seen Isabelle was safe, left us to do reconnaissance, making sure they had all the bad guys rounded up and all evidence of this night wiped out. He poked his head into the room to tell me that all was clear, and he was ready to do the cleanup.

I carried Isabelle out to the car and buckled her in. Jax had asked if he could come back with us. With a nod from Isabelle, he jumped in his car. Isabelle was silent on the car ride home. I wouldn't push her, allowing her to talk when she was ready. She'd been through a nightmare; all I wanted now was to get her home to safety.

Chapter 23

Isabelle

Steve, Marshall, and I walked out of Alan's studio on cloud nine. We'd had the best day of our lives. Not only had we met our musical heroes, but we had jammed with them as well. We learned more in one day then in the last year.

Working with the upper echelons of the music industry had its advantages. I could see how music shows like The Voice would have such a significant impact on a person's career. Not only the mentoring but being around and absorbing the knowledge from 'musicpreneurs' was so impactful. We had a home, a new music family.

"Come on, Isabelle, just one drink," the guys begged.

I laughed and looked at the car waiting for me. "Let's set up something for after work tomorrow. The car is waiting, which means Iver is waiting. I'll see you tomorrow; have fun without me," I said while sticking out my tongue. They both flipped me off and sauntered over to their ride. I laughed and made my way to mine.

I was surprised that Benson was not already out of the car to open my door. Usually, when he saw me coming, he would get out of the vehicle with a big smile on his face. As I got closer, I felt the hairs on the back of my neck rise.

Something wasn't right. Then the driver got out of the car and opened my door. I hesitated and pulled out my phone to text Iver, to make sure he had sent the car for me. Before I could type him a message, I was grabbed from behind and thrown in the car. I fought, and I may have gotten out, but a rag soaked in something that smelled disgusting pressed over my face.

When I woke up, I was sitting, tied to a chair in a living room. I moved my eyes around the room. My heart sunk with despair when I realized where I was. I groaned and tried moving my hands. The bindings were too tight to loosen.

I tried moving my feet, the same story. I wasn't getting out of these, not without help. I didn't hear anyone in the house with me and almost had heart failure when someone grabbed my hair and yanked my head back. My neck snapped and I felt nerve pain radiating from my neck up into my face.

That was the least of my problems. Staring down into my eyes, was Robert Voss, my worst nightmare. Even though I was no longer a kid, being in my childhood home with my rapist sent me into a spiral. Tears leaked from the corners of my eyes, the only outward sign I gave of my struggle and fear.

The eyes that looked at me were not human; they were something else. I had a feeling Robert was one of the fallen or descended from the fallen.

He read my thoughts; he must have, for he chuckled, and his chuckle was not human. I literally felt my blood freeze in my veins. Robert's face morphed into a hideous mask. "You're right, young one, I am more than I have appeared to the mere mortals of this pathetic planet. I am Asmodeus, the demon of lust and destroyer of hope."

He suddenly let go of my head, which snapped back into place, and moved to sit on the couch opposite my chair, morphing back to Robert Voss as he did. I was in big shit; he was going to kill me. But if he did, wouldn't that kill him or at least make him mortal? Isn't that what Iver had said?

Again, the demon Asmodeus read my thoughts. "Your angel is wrong, little immortal. I was never part of the fallen. I am already a demon from the depths of Hell, far below where we currently are. A realm that is run by a master who is the master of illusion. Your pathetic beliefs can't stand a chance against one as strong as my master."

I needed to buy time. If I thought about Iver, this piece of dung would pick up on it, so instead, I focused all my mental energy on Asmodeus. If I fanned his ego and all my thoughts were of him, he would read only that. Maybe I could keep him busy long enough for Iver to find me.

"So, why me, then? If my death doesn't do anything to you, then why bother with me? And why remain in your pathetic disguise if your master is all-powerful?" This was my attempt at deflecting him from my fear, while behind me, I dug my fingernails into my sensitive palms.

I kept pushing. "Why bother with Robert Voss? Why not just be who you are, if you're not of the fallen and you are not worried about death? If I can't kill you or make you mortal, then why disguise yourself as that piece of shit?"

His demonic chuckle made the hairs on my arms stand at attention. "In answer to your question, I saw you, Isabelle. I saw your light, and I couldn't help myself. I had to have it. I had to take your virginity and destroy you. Feeling your love and happiness give way to fear and despair, was like candy in my mouth; you were truly delicious."

"Well, I won't be tasting so delicious this time, buddy. I have had immortal sex with a fallen, and he is so much better than you at fucking." I was playing with fire, but I thought if I pissed him off, it would take his mind off killing me quickly and give Iver time to find me.

"I told you to watch the outside," Asmodeus commanded. The other man nodded and went back outside. He looked like a robot, unthinking, on autopilot. "He is possessed to follow my every order. If I told him to stab himself, he would. I plan on killing him when I'm done with you."

Sweat trickled down my back as his words sunk in. "Oh? Are you afraid of little ol' me, Asmodeus?"

He was still in his Robert meat suit, but I could see the beast through his crazy eyes. It was his eyes that had so affected me as a young girl. They seemed soulless, and now I knew why. "I am not afraid of you, angel girl, but you should be very, very afraid of me."

I laughed like a maniac, staring into his red eyes. "I am not afraid of you, demon; you are nothing. You're not even free. You are a slave to your master, to your lust. You are nothing and not worth my fear or anything else."

Now I'd pissed him off. He stood, with real steam coming out of his ears. He stomped the few steps toward me and back-handed me, sending the chair flying backward. I felt myself being lifted and carried into another room, then nothing.

I woke within minutes; I was sure of it. Now I was tied to a bed, facedown. Shit, I was so vulnerable. Tears began to leak out from the corners of my eyes as I realized that I probably wouldn't make it out alive. I felt Asmodeus in the room somewhere behind, watching me.

Then he was straddling me, his thighs draped over my legs. He leaned down and whispered in my ear. "You know, Isabelle, you may no longer be a virgin, but I know of a place where you have yet to be touched. Maybe before I kill you, I will take that from you too."

Oh my god! I tried closing my legs, but the ropes he had tied around my ankles held fast. He got off me and unzipped his pants. I closed my eyes and begged God, archangel Michael, and anyone else who may be listening to please help me.

Then I heard a crash that sounded like a pot falling in the kitchen. Asmodeus swore in anger. He leaned over and gave my behind such a hard slap, I knew a bruise of his handprint would be evident on my white skin. I yelped, and he laughed, leaving me and making his way toward the kitchen.

I held my breath in anticipation. *Please be Iver, please.* Suddenly, a sense of peace came over me. Opening my eyes, I saw Iver at the window. He held his finger to his lips, and I blinked in acknowledgment.

Asmodeus walked back in. I panicked and began bucking in my restraints. Iver jumped through the window and grabbed a surprised Robert Voss and ripped his head clean off. A moment later, I heard the splintering of wood coming from the living room.

Iver was untying the knots that held me with speed I didn't think possible, and in seconds I was pulled to his chest and encapsulated in the safety of his arms. As I inhaled his scent, I knew I was safe. The floodgates opened, and I let the tears of relief fall.

"It's okay now, Bella, I have you, and Robert can't hurt you ever again."

I cried and cried with relief. I was safe; now I could let go of everything that had happened. I hid in Iver's chest, not wanting to let go, not ever.

Chapter 24

Iver

"Asmodeus," she uttered when we were almost to the penthouse. I glanced at Isabelle, who was staring straight ahead with empty eyes. She was lost somewhere, and I couldn't help her until I could park the damn car.

I pulled into the parking garage, Jax right behind me. I lifted Isabelle out of the car and carried her to my private elevator, the ride quiet, no one saying a word. Once upstairs, I placed her on the couch, leaving her wrapped up.

We hadn't found her purse or clothing, guessing her kidnappers thought there might be tracers. He'd probably tossed them, along with the phones. I looked at the giant bruise on her face and asked her to open and close her mouth a few times. Once I made sure her jaw was not broken or dislocated, I grabbed an ice pack from the freezer.

She struggled to sit up higher, and I handed her a glass of water. Placing her head back into the cushions, she noticed Jax for the first time. "Hi," she said as she tried to smile, but it failed, instead, appearing as a grimace.

Jax dropped to his knees beside her, taking her cold, white hand in his. "How are you, Isabelle? Are you okay? He didn't do anything, did he?"

"No, Jax, my heroes arrived just in time. He'd walked into the room to rape me before killing me. He'd just unzipped his pants when we heard a crash from the direction of the kitchen, then Iver leaped through the window."

She licked her lips, and I held the water glass to her mouth. "I think a round of your best scotch is in order, Iver."

We all laughed, her humor working as a restorative tonic for all of us. An hour and three more shots of scotch later, I asked Jax to stay and to invite his brother Finn to join us, while I bathed Isabelle and put her to bed. I saw the large paw print that the animal, Asmodeus, had left behind. I wished I could go back and kill him over again.

I needed to get out of that mindset and use my energy to implement new measures and not just for Isabelle. The demon realm knew of Isabelle's existence, and once they learned of the extinction of one their powerful dark lords, no doubt they would send another.

Back in the living room, Jax refilled our glasses, and sitting with him on the couch was brother number two, Finn. It had been a long night already. My body craved the warmth of the beauty in my bed, but for now, I shut off my needs so I could work a few things out with the brothers and explain the dangers we would all be facing.

Finn looked at me and then to Jax. "What is going on? Who are you? Who the hell is Asmodeus, and why was a demon after my sister?"

I sighed and rubbed my hand over my face. Jax keeping Finn entirely ignorant had probably seemed wise at the time, but after tonight, he would know everything, and I hoped the gentle empath had enough strength to deal with it.

"Finn, what do you know of the fallen?" His look said it all

—nothing. I looked at Jax and shook my head. "Listen, much of what you are going to hear may sound too fantastic to be real. But I assure you it is all true, and Jax can confirm much of it."

He glanced at his brother for confirmation. Jax nodded, and I continued. For the next two hours, I talked about the fallen, God, Enoch, Ariella, and how I came to be with Isabelle. I even talked more about lineage and gifts that came from the mating of two fallen and the possibility of Finn having immortal genes.

Jax had been wrestling with something during my little speech, and finally, he spoke up. "Iver, I met someone at the Renaissance Ball. Her name is Lillith, and she said she works for you. Is she an immortal?"

"Before I answer that, Jax, our conversations must stay between us, family only. Most of the fallen's descendants have no idea what they are or, if they do, are unaware of the others unless they meet. Descendants have a natural attraction for each other. Did you feel a strong pull, an attraction for Lillith? Beyond the sex, do you feel the need to spend every moment of the day with her? Feeling jealous when you shouldn't, and most importantly, when you had sex, did you use protection?"

Jax shifted in his seat, looking suddenly uncomfortable with the questions I asked him. "Um, yes, to all of the above, but with regards to sex, she is on the pill, so we didn't use a condom. And, well, when we orgasmed, I saw things. I was in outer space, looking down on our planet, and I saw everything, the beginning, the millennium of subtle shifts in the earth, and the environment. I saw empires rise and fall, and millions of years of Earth pass in seconds. I thought I was dreaming, but in the morning, Lillith shared her dreams with me, and they were the same. How is that possible?"

"She is one of the descendants of the fallen. I know her family, and her grandfather is unaware of her immortality, as it comes from her mother's side. Her mother's ancestors have all married humans, and most of them died without ever knowing what they were."

Finn looked confused. "Does this immortality only come from the women's side?"

"Yes, and no," I answered. "If two immortals have mated, their offsprings' immortal genes come from both sides. In answer to your question, Jax, yes, Lillith is an immortal, and so are you. The only reason you were unaware of it is you are not a direct descendant of Ariella; you are in her line, as we discussed the other day. You share the same lineage on your mother's side with Isabelle."

Finn and Jax both sat back, sipping their scotch in silence. I decided to continue along this line of lineage. Finn needed to know that he and Jax were not Isabelle's birth brothers.

"I am one of the original descendants, and my mother is the goddess Freya. I was born as I am, utterly aware of my heritage and parentage, and so is Isabelle. Her mother was Ariella, and her father is Apollo."

When the meaning of my words sunk in, Finn sputtered his scotch. If the topic of our conversation hadn't been so intense, I would have been laughing. "Isabelle is not your real sister and is the head of Ariella's lineage now. As you know already, Jax, she is the savior."

I glanced at my soon to be brother-in-law. "In your case, Jax, if you and Lillith decide to bond and mate for life, both your genes will be passed on to your offspring, live and active because of your many times removed demigod genes from Apollo. Lillith, if she mated with a lesser descendant, would only pass on immortality to her offspring, assuming she had them activated.

"And activation happens how again?" asked Finn.

"An original fallen passed their knowledge to their mate through sex. The essence lies in creation. You know the birds and the bees; your little swimmers are magic. Mothers mated to another immortal pass it along in their breastmilk. There have been many unfortunate immortals who died because their activation never happened, for one reason or another. Now, Jax is activated through sexual relations with an immortal. There is another way. The fallen, or their direct offspring, can wake up dormant genes in others. In your case, Finn, if you don't meet up with an immortal female or ask me to activate you, then you will remain mortal; the choice is yours."

Finn grinned. "So the only downside to all of this is, what? That some of the fallen are jealous assholes and want to kill off the good fallen?"

Jax cut in here. "Finn, for us, eternity may look like a forever picnic and opportunity to create untold wealth, like Iver. If something happens to Isabelle, then the future of the fallen and their descendants change; they become mortal and die. Iver and Isabelle are the keys to immortality continuing on Earth."

Finn looked genuinely concerned for his sister. I liked this brother; his empath ability was his dominant power. He was like an aphrodisiac. If he were to meet an immortal female, she would be strongly attracted to his pheromones.

"In other words, if Isabelle dies in the next nine hundred and eighty years, we all die."

Finn sat back, blowing out a long breath. "That's a tough gig, and Issy knows this?"

I nodded. "She does."

"And what are you to her, then?"

I chuckled. "Beyond being a man entirely in love, I am her protector, I was charged by the archangel Michael to ensure that she lives and that we create offspring. In 980 years, when Isabelle gives birth to a girl, the curse placed upon the fallen will be rescinded, and once again, we can walk the earth and the heavenly realms in equal measure. Our immortality will no longer be a gift to be feared, but a gift to be revered."

Finn was quietly digesting the information I'd been sharing for the last few hours.

"Listen," I said, standing up. "We have lots of time to discuss the pros and cons, and we need a conversation about security. But for now, I'm going to sleep with my woman and hopefully keep the nightmares away."

Jax stood. "I didn't know she had nightmares."

"Really, Jax?" Finn said, rolling his eyes exactly like his sister. "Like since she was eleven. Didn't you ever notice?"

Jax shook his head, looking embarrassed. "I guess not."

I decided to leave before I said something rude to Jax. "Your bedrooms are down the hall, on the left. Good night, gentlemen."

"Good night, Iver, and thank you," Finn said, shaking my hand, "for keeping Issy safe. She needs you."

"That she does," I agreed and left them in the hall to decide which rooms they wanted—closing my bedroom door softly.

I undressed in the bathroom and had a shower before hopping into bed. I played over Asmodeus' role in the taking down of the immortals. He must have been kicking himself when he found out later that the same girl he'd tormented was the savior, I mused during my shower. I'd heard of the demon; I knew of all the head demons, by name only. But I needed to know more and what to expect.

After breakfast with the brothers, I would take Isabelle to Silicon Valley to meet with Egan, our historian, and then to Africa, to talk to my father. Enoch had returned to Africa in the year 2000, for quiet contemplation. He should have been here with me, helping to identify Ariella's descendant.

But I get it. Like all the original, Enoch was extremely fearful despite the vast power he had. The death of my mother shadowed all of his actions and thoughts. It was time to pull my father out of the past. I needed him and his power to help me keep Isabelle safe.

As I gently moved in behind her in bed, she sighed and snuggled her backside into me. I wrapped her in the safety of my arms and, moments later, sunk into a deep sleep.

The next day, as we boarded my jet bound for Los Angeles, Isabelle looked at me. "Thank you, Iver."

"For what, my love?"

"For being right all along. I did need a protector, and I'm glad it's you."

The End

Skylar West

Skylar West is a Canadian writer, new on the author scene and making a big impact with her steamy romance books. She loves walks in the rain, hot cups of delicious java, overly large sweaters, and the type of steamy sex she writes about in her novels. A cat lover, this author looks forward to writing many more novels.

Find her on Facebook: https://www.facebook.com/sky. west.1806

Don't miss these exciting titles by Skylar West and Blushing Books!

Fallen Angel
Marked
The Dark Side of Kingsley